Karen King is an experienced writing tutor and university lecturer on professional and university writing courses and has been writing children's books since the mid-eighties. She's written for many children's magazines including *Sindy Barbie*, *Winnie the Pooh* and *Thomas the Tank E...* stories ... re featured on BBC's *Playdays* and her poems on the BBC *One Potato, Two Potato* website. She writes for all ages and in all genres: story books, picture books, plays, joke books, she's written them all! She currently tutors for The Writer's Bureau and was one of the authors of their Writing for Children course and the author of their Write for Profit using the Internet course.

Other titles from How To Books

HOW TO WRITE A CHILDREN'S PICTURE BOOK
and get it published
Andrea Shavick

365 WAYS TO GET YOU WRITING
Daily inspiration and advice for creative writers
Jane Cooper

CHOOSE THE RIGHT WORD
*An entertaining and easy-to-use guide to better English – with
70 test-yourself quizzes*
Robin Hosie and Vic Mayhew

HOW TO WRITE YOUR FIRST NOVEL
Sophie King

THE FIVE-MINUTE WRITER
Exercise and inspiration in creative writing in five minutes a day
Margret Geraghty

Get Writing Children's Fiction

Karen King

howtobooks

Constable & Robinson Ltd
55-56 Russell Square
London WC1B 4HP
www.constablerobinson.com

First published in the UK by How To Books,
an imprint of Constable & Robinson Ltd., 2013

A copy of the British Library Cataloguing in Publication
Data is available from the British Library

ISBN 978-1-8452-8506-7 (paperback)
ISBN 978-1-4721-1013-8 (ebook)

Printed and bound in the UK

1 3 5 7 9 10 8 6 4 2

Contents

Contents

Contents

Contents

Acknowledgements

Massive thanks to the many people who gave me quotes for this book, mainly members of the hugely supportive Scattered Authors Society (SAS). Thanks especially to: Ann Evans, Jackie Marchant, Wendy Meddour, Diana Kimpton, John Ward, Leila Rasheed, Linda Strachan, Alan Cliff, David Calcutt, John Dougherty, Nick Catman, Sandra Glover, Nicola Morgan and Moira Butterfield.

Is This You?

Are you burning with the desire to create stories that children will want to read time and time again? To transport them into fantasy worlds, exciting adventures, realistic family dramas? To entertain children, make them laugh or shiver with fright? To create characters they can relate to and care about? Do you have children's stories buzzing around in your head, fighting to get out and down on paper? If you can answer yes to any of these questions then this is the book for you. Between these covers you will learn the techniques needed to create believable characters, realistic dialogue and gripping plots for children plus useful writing tips and exercises. So dip inside and get writing!

1

Writing for Children 'Know-how'

BEFORE STARTING

Children are not mini adults; they are a totally different audience. So before you start writing a children's story, think about some of the differences between children and adults. Let's discuss a few and how it will affect your writing:

+ *Children are younger and less experienced.* Their knowledge is more limited than adults so make sure that you write about things they will understand. Think about the age of the child who will be reading your story. We'll talk more about this later in the chapter.

+ *Children are smaller.* Have you ever been back to your primary school and realized with shock how small it actually is? Remember how huge the school seemed when you were a child? It was easy to get lost there, the desks were high, the teachers tall, everything seemed so big. Try getting down on your knees to see the world through a child's eyes. See how high the table is, how impossible it is to reach the shelf, how tall adults seem. Bear this in mind when you're writing your story.

+ *Children's vocabulary and understanding aren't as developed as adults.* It's amazing how many authors write a children's story just as they would write a story for adults but with children as the characters. Use vocabulary relevant to your age group and don't put anything in the story that a child of that age wouldn't understand.

+ *Children are impressionable.* Children have limited experience. They haven't been in this world as long as adults. To young children anything is possible. They will happily believe that toys come to life, animals can talk and fairies exist. Which brings us to the next, very important, point.

WRITING RESPONSIBLY

Never forget how impressionable children are, especially children under seven. The world is new and fresh to them and their knowledge is limited. They can be influenced by what they read and will often copy a scenario, basing themselves on one of the characters. So write responsibly. *Never* show young children doing any of the following:

+ Talking to strangers.

+ Going off with strangers.

+ Wandering about alone or going off alone.

+ Doing anything that could cause them harm.

Getting past 'the gatekeepers'

If you want to be published in the traditional way then your story probably won't get past an editor if you do any of the above things. If you are writing a children's story, before your book even reaches its target audience it has to get past what is known in the trade as 'the gatekeepers'. These are editors, publishers, critics, educationalists and librarians who all check that the content of the story is suitable for children of the age for which it is intended. Stories featuring children having unsupervised adventures like Enid Blyton's *Famous Five* wouldn't be acceptable today. Hence the rise of fantasy fiction: put your child in a fantasy world and you can relax the barriers a little.

A warning tale

Editors can be very cautious, especially with books aimed at children under five. Several publishers told me that they loved my picture book story *Silly Moo!* but they wouldn't publish it because they considered it too dangerous – in the story an apple falls on Cow's head and she forgets where she lives. Their concern was that the book would encourage children to throw apples, or other things, at each other's heads. I personally felt that was a bit over the top. I finally sold *Silly Moo!* to Top That! Publishing who didn't think it was too dangerous at all and turned it into a colourful lift-the-flap book which is very popular with children.

> ### Top tip
> A general rule of thumb is that children must never be shown doing anything that children would not safely be allowed to do in real life.

CONSIDERING OTHER THINGS

Some general rules for all age groups are:

+ *Make sure that your book isn't sexist.* Don't portray boys as always being stronger, braver or tougher than girls. Don't show girls as always being kinder, more patient or cleverer than boys. Characters of both sexes have their own individual strengths and weaknesses.

+ *Don't stereotype characters.* Don't always show your male characters doing stereotypically male things such as playing football or larking around and your female characters playing ballet or simpering. All Africans aren't good at athletics, all Asians aren't shopkeepers and studious, and all Scots don't have ginger hair. Most women now go out to work and some men are househusbands. I once had to rewrite a short story because I'd shown the mum washing up and the dad at work. "But I do wash up, don't you?" I asked my editor. "Yes," she replied. "But that's not the point."

+ *Reflect the society we live in.* We live in a diverse, multicultural society consisting of a variety of lifestyles, family structures, homes, customs and ways of dressing. Make sure your story reflects this. Don't always portray your characters as a middle-class white nuclear family with mum, dad and two children. There are many single-parent families – and there are single-parent dads as well as mums – step-families, mixed race families and family members with a disability.

Warning!

Don't overdo the points above. Making your character a working-class, ballet-loving boy living with a disabled single-parent dad and six siblings from different races won't guarantee that your story is an instant success with your editor.

WRITING ABOUT ISSUES

Obviously, the older the child you are writing for, the more the rules slacken. For pre-teens you should never write anything immoral or containing bad language, but this is less true for teenage books, which are more commonly known as YA (Young Adult) fiction. Controversial subjects such as teenage pregnancy (*A Swift Pure Cry* by Siobhan Dowd), suicide (*Thirteen Reasons Why* by Jay Asher), drug-taking (*Junk* by Melvin Burgess) and even incest (*Forbidden* by Tabitha Suzuma) occur in these titles, which can result in them being banned by schools and librarians.

Most YA authors say they write about these issues because these are problems teenagers have to deal with, and they hope that in some way their stories can help them. I'm with them on this; as long as the subjects are tackled responsibly (i.e. not encouraging readers to do it or written in a sensational, vulgar way) then I think there is definitely a place for these kinds of stories. Life, as the saying goes, is not a bed of roses and by the time they get to their teens most children know this.

Of course, not all books today are traditionally published. The rise of self e-publishing sites such as Amazon Kindle and

Smashwords means that an ever-increasing number of writers are taking that route instead. If you intend to self-publish then remember that even though you don't have an editor you still have a responsibility to consider the age of your audience and write accordingly. We'll talk more about ebooks and self-publishing in chapter 14.

All these points are obvious really, yet it's amazing how many writers forget these basics and write just the same as they would for adults. A children's story is for children so your subject matter, theme and vocabulary should reflect this.

> **Top tip**
>
> Always remember the audience you are writing for – this is good advice for any writer but especially important for a writer of children's fiction.

Writing exercise

Think of a children's book you read as a child. How did it make you feel? If you were writing that story now what would you change about it? Have a go at tweaking the plot to make it more modern (and more PC, if necessary). Rewrite the first page or two. What difference does it make to the story?

KNOWING YOUR MARKET, KNOWING YOUR READER

'Know you market, know your reader' is a mantra that I often tell my students. I believe that this is vital when writing for children.

Researching the market

I've often heard it said that you should just write the book you want to write and if it's written well enough it will find a home. Personally I don't agree with this. Children's publishing is very market-led, publishers have their own quotas and lists they want to fill, and whilst I don't recommend you jump on the bandwagon and write what's 'hot' at the moment, I do recommend you research what's already out there and what current editors are looking for.

If you want to get your book published you need to be aware of the current market, if only to ensure that you're not writing something similar to a story that's already on sale. A look at a selection of publishers' websites will inform you of books that have been around for a while but are still popular as well as current titles and forthcoming ones. You'll also be able to find information on the various series the publishers commission and be able to download a catalogue of all current book titles. This is all useful information as publishers often look for books to fit into their series.

Be aware that although books like *Postman Pat*, *Bob the Builder*, *The Secret Seven* and other Enid Blyton titles are still popular, stories like these wouldn't get past an editor today. Publishers are looking for modern stories with plots that reflect the society children now live in. They are not looking for cute, twee, old-fashioned characters such as Sammy Suitcase or Tommy Toothbrush, hackneyed storylines ending with 'it was all a dream' or fantasy stories where a whisk of the wand magically solves every problem.

However, if you have a story that's really burning in your head, just waiting to be written down, then go ahead, write it. You may have to wait a while to get it published but some of the best stories have been written by authors who had a story they simply had to tell. Before J. K. Rowling's first *Harry Potter* book, publishers and agents were saying that boarding-school stories were 'old hat', but Rowling came up with a unique setting and characters and the rest is history. Do make sure, though, that you write your story for today's children, and show the characters using modern language and living in the world as it is now, unless, of course, it's a historical or fantasy story. I see a lot of manuscripts from writers whose stories sound dated because their characters act and speak like children did fifty years ago. In other words, write the story that you're itching to write but make sure that it fits in with today's society.

> **Top tip**
>
> Read lots of modern children's books so you can get a feel for the characters and plots that are popular now. Reading is almost as important as writing for a children's author.

Knowing your reader

It's vital that you think about the age of the child for whom you're writing and at what genre/market you're aiming. Obviously, the age of your reader will affect the way you write your story as a five-year-old will require a simpler story plot, vocabulary and sentence structure than a nine-year-old. Of course, this is only a general observation; there are five-year-olds with the reading ability of eight-year-olds and vice versa, but it's something you should bear in mind.

The age of your reader will also determine the length of your story as publishers tend to organize their lists according to age groups, with the books for each age group being different word lengths. The age range and length can differ from publisher to publisher, and only by researching individual publishers' lists will you learn the requirements of each one. If the guidelines aren't available on the publisher's website write and ask for them, enclosing a stamped addressed envelope, of course. Here is a general guide.

WRITING FOR DIFFERENT AGE GROUPS

Writing for pre-school children

Books for pre-schoolers are often the ones most people think are the easiest to write. Don't be fooled. These short, illustrated books might look simple but it's a difficult and highly competitive market for which to write. Books for this age group usually fall into three types:

Baby board books. These can have as little as one word per page and are primarily educational to teach the child to identify the picture with the word. Openings for new writers are few and far between as they are usually written in-house by editors or commissioned out to well-known artists.

Toddler books. These tell a simple story that the child can identify with (such as remembering to use the potty/being scared of the dark/not wanting to go to bed) and are around 250 words long. The trick to writing these is to keep the story simple and to use the illustrations to tell the story as much as possible – this is known in the trade as 'letting the pictures do the talking'.

Picture books. The most popular book for pre-schoolers. Again these tell a simple story with a beginning, middle and end based around situations with which children can identify but with a fresh, original take such as *Can't You Sleep, Little Bear?* by Martin Waddell (dealing with being scared of the dark), *Where the Wild Things Are* by Maurice Sendak (a child's anger) and *I Want My Potty!* by Tony Ross (even princesses have to be potty trained). Picture books are a maximum of 1,000 words, preferably 500 words or fewer. Picture-book characters can be children, animals, toys or fantasy characters but they should all appeal to young children.

Writing for five- to six-year-olds

Children of this age are just starting to read on their own and enjoy both picture books and first readers. First readers are standard 'paperback size' and 1,500–2,000 words. The stories usually have a simple storyline that can be zany or contemporary, without flashbacks or long sentences, and have an illustration on every page.

Writing for six- to seven-year-olds

Books for this age group are a transition between first readers and chapter books. They are about 4,000 words in length and often form part of a series. They are highly illustrated, usually with small black-and-white pictures. Action-packed stories are popular, broken into short chapters that end on a page-turner. Characters should be credible and there should be plenty of dialogue, but descriptive narrative should be kept to a minimum.

Writing for seven- to nine-year-olds

Series are very popular with this age group and the books are now about 10,000 words in length. Children of this age are more confident readers so vocabulary isn't so restricted and sentences are longer. Use strong characters, lots of dialogue and action. Black-and-white illustrations usually appear every couple of pages and again the story is told in chapters.

Children, especially boys aged between about six and nine, love funny stories with zany characters – think *There's a Pharaoh in Our Bath* by Jeremy Strong, the *Horrid Henry* series or the *Astrosaurs Academy* series. These books are popular with girls too, as are 'girly' series such as *Rainbow Magic* and *The Secret Kingdom*.

Writing for nine- to twelve-year-olds

This is the age of the avid reader. Children of this age are usually fluent readers and like to immerse themselves in a book. Fantasy, horror, sci-fi and humour are popular themes, as are series of up to ten books or more involving the same characters. The length of these books varies from 25,000 words upwards, and there are subplots and twists and turns to the story to keep the readers' interest. There can be several minor characters but the main character must always be in the foreground, and the story told through their eyes. The *Harry Potter* books are the obvious example for this age group, but there's also *Artemis Fowl* by Eoin Colfer and the Jacqueline Wilson books, which are very popular with girls.

Writing YA fiction

Young Adult or teenage fiction has been particularly popular in the last few years. At the time of writing this book, the 'black covers' of the *Twilight* and other vampire/horror series are predominant on the shelves of the bookstores. Books can vary between 40,000 and 80,000 words. Romance, contemporary, humour and horror are again popular, with stories often being told from more than one character's viewpoint – although each character usually has their own chapter so there is a clear division between them.

Writing exercise

Write the first paragraph of a story from the point of view of a five-year-old. Then write it from the point of view of a nine-year-old and finally that of a teenager. What differences did you make to the sentence structure and vocabulary? Which age group did you find it easiest to write for?

Top tip

If you're struggling with your story, consider whether you're writing it for the right age group. Play around with it for a while, trying out beginnings for a few different ages to see which one flows better. A lot of people have a certain age group in mind that they'd like to write for but their writing style is actually more suitable for younger/older children.

STUDYING GENRES

If you have a particular genre you would like to write for – fantasy or horror perhaps – then do study several books in this genre. See how established authors tackle the characters, settings, motifs and vocabulary. Motifs are things that are familiar to and define each genre, such as a typical character, setting or event. A zombie character, for example, indicates a horror story, a fairy suggests a fantasy story and an alien a sci-fi story.

Genres, of course, can be mixed and overlap; many sci-fi books have some horror or fantasy in them and vice versa.

WRITING ABOUT WHAT INTERESTS YOU

Don't attempt to write for a genre unless you are a fan of that genre. If you hate horror films and books, your attempts at writing them aren't likely to be very successful. To write science fiction you need to do some research and to have some knowledge of technology and how it might advance. Writing fantasy may seem an easier option as you can create an imaginary world and your own rules, but your plot must still be feasible, your fantasy world credible, your characters believable and any magic used must have a source and limitations to its use – your reader will soon lose interest if your 'Key Character' merely whips out his wand to magic away any problem he encounters.

ENTERTAINING NOT EDUCATING

The most important thing to remember when writing a children's story is that it should be entertaining. Many writers believe that a children's story should contain some lesson or moral and write with the purpose of 'educating' their young audience. Don't. Children go to school to be educated; when they pick up a story book they want it to be just that – a story. They want to be entertained, to laugh, to cry, to shiver with fear, to hold their breath in anticipation, to be transported to new worlds. Of course, many stories do have a moral and message in them but this should come about as the result of the story, not the reason for it. When you're writing for children the story is the most important thing. And it should never be preachy, mediocre or boring. Children deserve the very best you can write.

SUMMING UP

+ Write children's fiction only if those are the stories you really want to write.

+ Remember the age of your reader and write responsibly.

+ Familiarize yourself with what children like to read.

+ Write in language children can identify with and understand.

+ Entertain! Children like to read for fun.

2

Ideas Are All Around You

A WORLD OF IDEAS

One of the most common questions I get asked is, 'Where do you get your ideas from?' I always reply that I never have a problem getting ideas for stories. The problem is having time to write up all my ideas!

Ideas are all around you. Everyday life is full of the stuff that makes stories: things getting lost, plans going wrong, arguments, disasters, birthdays and parties are all good fodder for the writing mind. Simply think about how a child would cope with the problem or incident and you have the basis of a story. Here are just a few real-life situations to get you started:

An argument. Think about an argument you've had with one of your children; if you haven't got children think of an argument you had with a sibling or friends when you were young. Now write about it from *their* point of view. Imagine how they felt, what they thought, why they said the things they did. Thinking about something from someone else's viewpoint can be good writing practice. Often when you're struggling with a story it can be because you're writing from the wrong viewpoint: it's the other character's story you should be telling. We'll talk a little more about this later in the book.

The worst birthday ever. We've all planned birthday parties or treats for our children that haven't gone according to plan. Maybe one of your childhood birthdays went drastically wrong, or you were disappointed not to get the present for which you hoped. Writing about it will get the creative juices going and might even give you an idea for a story. If you haven't got a bad birthday memory – lucky you! – make one up.

An ideal day. Imagine one of your children, or yourself as a child, had a whole day to do whatever they wanted. Money is no object. What would they do? Where would they go? Who would they go with? What would happen? This is a great exercise for 'getting into the head' of your character.

All three of these exercises can be used either to get you writing or as a basis for a children's story.

WRITING EVERY DAY

To be a writer you need to write, it's as simple as that. So try to get into the habit of writing every day. This doesn't mean that you have to write reams of stuff – just a short paragraph will suffice. It's a good idea to keep a special journal where you can jot down any thoughts and ideas that come to you as well as notes on your day. If you're out and about you could use your smartphone to write down or record your ideas. This will get you into the habit of writing and stir up your creative juices, which should make it easier to think of story ideas.

WRITING ABOUT YOUR TYPICAL DAY

Just have a think about your typical day for a moment and write a quick checklist of the things you do. It might read something like this:

+ Go to work.

+ Look after your children.

+ Go shopping.

+ Meet friends for a coffee/drink/ or go to the gym/theatre/ cinema.

+ Do some gardening/other hobbies.

All these people and places can provide ideas for a story. Sometimes even writing down what you have done during the day can be enough to get you writing. Let's work through the above list and see how your typical day can inspire you.

Going to work

Going to work might sometimes seem a waste of your valuable writing time but it can actually enhance your writing. When you go to work you are mixing with people and are involved in situations that you won't encounter if you work from home every day. This interaction with people can stimulate ideas for stories, whilst the working environment itself could come in very handy when writing your children's novel. Another bonus is that there's nothing like having to fit in your writing during your work break or for an hour each morning and evening, before and after work, to make you focus. Writers who have all day to write might take just that, with a lot of the time spent daydreaming, web-surfing, tweeting, etc.

Writing exercise

Here are three writing exercises you could do based around your work:

1 *Describe your office or the view from your office window, using as many descriptive phrases as possible.*

2 *Think of all the people who work with you. They all have families. Now imagine the life of the children of someone who does a completely different job to you – the director, perhaps. Write a short paragraph describing what you think their child's life would be like.*

3 *Imagine taking a child to work with you for the day. Do you think they would like your job? Write a short diary extract from a child's point of view of a day at your workplace. This is a good exercise for thinking about things from a child's perspective.*

Top tip

Do a writing exercise every day to get you into the habit of writing.

Looking after children

The things children say and do can be a constant source of inspiration. Several of my children's books have been inspired by things that my children or grandchildren have done. I got the ideas for my picture book *I Don't Eat Toothpaste Anymore!* and first reader *The Gold Badge* from incidents involving one of my daughters. Looking after my grandson for the day inspired my picture book *And Me!* and another daughter was the inspiration for my book *Spider Spell.*

Writing exercise

Here are a few ways you can use incidents with your family to kick-start your writing. If you haven't got children then write the exercise from the point of view of a child you know.

1   Write down something the child has said that day. Now make that into the opening sentence of a children's story and free-write the first page. Don't think too much about this: go with the first idea that comes into your head. It could be something as simple as 'I can't find my gym kit'.

2   Think about a day out you had with your family and friends. Now imagine that you got lost on the way. Write about what happens from the child's point of view. Think about how the child would feel, what they would think or do.

3   Describe your house from the child's point of view. Get down on your knees to get a feel of how different things look to a child. Chairs and tables can seem enormous, for example, and they might not be able to reach the handle to open the door. Remember children's limited life experience, too — they won't understand what some things

are or what you do with them. This is an especially useful exercise to help you understand what the world looks like through a child's eyes.

Shopping

Whether you like shopping or not, it offers a wonderful opportunity for ideas. Think about all the people you meet – and, yes, some actually do seem to do their supermarket shopping in their pyjamas. The two old ladies quarrelling about who was first in the queue, the toddler grabbing the tin of beans from the middle of the display and bringing the whole lot crashing down, the husband and wife arguing in the middle aisle over what to have for dinner – all can be used as a springboard for a children's story if you simply add a child to the situation.

Writing exercise

1   *Write about your child character going shopping, while imagining that their parents are rich or have won the lottery so they have as much money as they want to spend. What shops would the child go into? What would they buy? Obviously the age of your character will have an influence on this.*

2   *Imagine what it would be like to work in a store like Harrods. Think about the customers you would meet. Now imagine being the child of one of them – a diplomat, celebrity or Saudi prince perhaps. What would your life be like?*

3   *Imagine you see a teenager shoplifting. Now think about why they are shoplifting. What is*

their life like? Are they doing it for a dare? Bullied into it? Stealing to feed the family because their mum or dad is ill or has walked out? A runaway trying to survive on the streets?

Meeting friends

Friends, like family, can be a constant source of ideas. I don't recommend that you write a story based on your friend's life or even use them as a character in a story – that would make you extremely unpopular, never mind the shaky legal ground you could be on if you wrote anything that could be deemed detrimental or libellous.

However, things they say and do can provide you with inspiration. You can use a true incident as the basis for a short story, changing the characters or the perspective so that it becomes something completely original. For example, if a friend is upset about her youngest child leaving home to go to university you could write a story based on this from the point of view of the teenager's younger sister or brother. How do they feel about the older brother or sister moving out? Do they get on with them? Are they looking forward finally to having a bedroom of their own? Do they resent their cleverer, prettier older sister/brother?

Writing exercise

1   *To write about children you need to know how they act and talk. So when you're out and about make mental notes of the mannerisms of any children you see. Note how they interact with*

each other, the facial expressions they pull, the things that attract them. You can then refer back to these notes when you're building up a character.

2   Screenwriting is visual so it is based more on showing than telling, a skill which can enhance your own work. When you go to the cinema or theatre notice how the characters speak — each character should have their own voice so you immediately know who's talking — and think about the visual effects in the film/play, how the writer has used them to tell the story. Make a few notes when you come home and try to 'show not tell' when you write a story.

3   Write about two children who are completely opposites but are best friends. Where did they meet? How did they become friends? Now imagine something happening that makes them fall out. Write a paragraph about the incident, first from one child's point of view then from the other child's perspective.

Top tip

Jot down snippets of any interesting dialogue you overhear. It might give you an idea for a story.

Enjoying hobbies

Most of us have things we like to do – cycling, gardening, photography or fishing, for instance – which all can provide material to get our imagination going. Simply sitting and observing our surroundings, listening to the different sounds, watching the birds fly around, noticing the many varieties of flowers and then writing about what we see is a good exercise.

Writing exercise

1   Describe your surroundings, noting what you see and hear. Now imagine the same scene in the middle of the night; write down what you would see and hear then. Compare the two scenes.

2   Write instructions for a child of twelve on how to do something connected with your hobby, such as the best flowers/vegetables to plant in each season, how to paint with watercolours or how to make cards. Now try writing out the instructions again for a child of nine and one of five. What difference is there between them? Did you use different language and vocabulary?

3   Imagine a child is interviewing you about your hobby, asking you questions such as what made you start doing it, why you like it and any tips you have. Write down the questions they might ask you and your replies. Try to make it sound as interesting as you can to them.

Top tip

Wherever you go, watch, observe, ask inner questions and jot down notes in your notebook. Your life is a constant source of inspiration. Use it.

WATCHING THE NEWS

Watching the news and reading newspapers or magazines can be another way of getting story ideas. A glance at today's headlines in a popular daily newspaper reveals the following stories: a house that is covered in ivy both inside and out; a village where things like showers, heating, door bells and even remote car key fobs have stopped working; and a girl who ran away when her boyfriend proposed at a basketball game. Any of these could be the foundation stone of an interesting story.

Writing exercise

1   Think about the house covered in ivy. How many families have lived there over the years? What events has the house seen? Pretend you are a child who lived in the house and write a diary about a typical day in your life.

2   Imagine that you live in a village where all the electrical things have stopped working. Write a short account from the point of view of a child.

3   Imagine that you were the teenage girl at the basketball game. How did you feel when your boyfriend proposed to you? Had you known him long? Did you love him? Why did you run away?

PEOPLE WATCHING

Do you hurry along, head bent, mind full of all the things you have to do? Well, lift up your head, look around and do a bit of 'people watching'. People can provide great ideas for stories.

See that couple sitting in the corner of the café, arguing? What are they arguing over? Are they married? On the brink of separation? Do they have children, how will this affect them?

What about the young boy dragging his feet as the woman holding his hand urges him along? Is she his mother? Stepmother? An aunt? Why is he so reluctant to go with her? And that group of teenagers hanging around the bench, what's their story? The girl with bright red hair or the boy with the blue cap, who are they? Do they get on with everyone in the group? What's their home life like? Use your imagination, jot down your ideas then go home and write up the one that interests you most.

Using overheard conversations

Ever been sitting on a bus or train and heard snippets of a really intriguing conversation, but the people have got off, or you've had to get off, before you could hear the full story? This has happened to me several times. I unashamedly admit that I find other people's conversations fascinating. Next time this happens to you, fill in the missing bits yourself. Write what you think happens next or what you think the conversation was about. Can you use it in a story? Perhaps they could be the parents of your child character.

Bus and train journeys not only give you time to watch – and listen to – people, they also supply you with a variety of characters that could be the inspiration for your next story. It could be the mum with the bottomless 'Mary Poppins' bag from which she pulls out item after item to soothe her fractious toddler, the old lady in the bright red jacket and lipstick who tells you she's on her way to meet an internet date, the man with the mobile phone seemingly glued to his ear as he makes 'deal after deal' during the journey. I travel by train a lot and have met many interesting characters who have given me countless ideas for stories – many of which I haven't written up yet. But I don't think anything beats the moment when a woman came running into the train carriage and shouted, 'Has anyone seen a pink folder with the name Amanda on it? It's got my early release papers from prison in it!' Now there's a story opening for you!

EXPANDING YOUR IDEAS

You might wonder what incidents like these have to do with writing children's stories. The answer is *everything*. Simply put a child in any of these situations and write from that child's point of view.

Imagine you are a child of the mother with the 'Mary Poppins' bag. Where are you going? Imagine that the lady with the red jacket is your grandmother, just divorced from your granddad and determined to 'live her life', that the man on the telephone was your workaholic dad, or that the lady with the pink folder was your mother just released from prison. How would you feel? Ask yourself, what's the child's story?

BRAINSTORMING YOUR IDEAS

Using 'What if . . . ?'

'What if...?' is one of the most effective methods of brainstorming, developing ideas and beating 'writer's block' that I know. Whenever you are stuck for an idea or can't seem to progress with your story, ask yourself 'What if . . . ?' What if your character found a bag full of money? What if they fancied their best friend's boyfriend or girlfriend? What if they discovered they were adopted? What if there was a thunderstorm? What if their magic stopped working? Carry on asking 'What if . . . ?' to help you build up the story or create more conflict.

SUMMING UP

+ Write something every day, even if it's only about what you can see from your window.

+ Wherever you are and whatever you do there is a potential story.

+ Always have a notebook and pencil with you to jot ideas down.

+ Look, listen and use all your senses.

+ Look out for anything unusual and jot it down.

3

Characters Make Stories

When I'm writing a story it's the character that comes to me first. A character pops into my head and starts 'talking' to me, then the storyline starts to form. The title often comes much later, sometimes when I've finished the whole book. Some people think of the storyline first, for others it's the title. We all work in different ways but whatever way we work it's the characters that are the most important ingredients in the story. If readers don't believe in your characters, relate to them and root for them then they won't care what happens to them. Credible characters are especially important for children's books because children lose interest quickly. No matter how fabulous and exciting your storyline is, children won't bother to finish it if they can't relate to your characters.

Children like to read about other children, the problems they face, the adventures they have and how they deal with things, so the main characters in children's books should be children, not adults. For pre-school children there is usually one main charac-ter (which I shall refer to as the Key Character) and one or two secondary characters. For example, in the popular picture book, *The Snail and the Whale* by Julia Donaldson, the snail is the main character and the whale is the secondary one. In fiction for five-year-olds and over there is often also a 'baddie', the antagonist, the one that causes our hero or heroine problems.

Let's take a look at these characters a bit more.

CHOOSING TYPES OF CHARACTERS

Establishing the Key Character

This is our hero/heroine, the character whose story we're telling. So this is the character your reader needs to believe in and relate to the most. Your Key Character should be introduced into your story right at the beginning and your reader will want to know a lot about them, especially their conflicts – both inner and outer – and desires.

> **Top tip**
>
> Children like to read about characters a little older than themselves so make your Key Character at the top end of your age range. For example, if your intended reader is five to seven, it's best to make your character seven to eight years old.

Establishing secondary characters

Obviously you'll want more than one character in your story, usually – but not always – the main character's family, friends, neighbours and other children at school. These characters might have quite an important part to play and feature heavily in the story but they should never overshadow the main character. You can name these characters and describe them a little so that the reader can easily identify them but don't go overboard. Keep the main focus on your Key Character.

Adding background characters

There will be several other characters in your story such as other pupils at school, neighbours and parents. There is no need to go into too much detail about these. Naming and describing several characters can be confusing for your reader and can take the focus away from the main character so keep your minor characters in the background where they belong.

Including adults

Whilst you will probably need some adults in your story, such as parents, teachers and other background characters, it's not a good idea to make an adult the main character. As I mentioned previously, children like to read about other child characters, not about adults and the problems they face. So keep your adult characters very much in the background.

Inventing fantasy characters

Fairies, elves, dragons, witches and wizards are all portrayed in storybooks. One of the advantages of using fantasy creatures is that they can get away with doing a lot more than real children, because they don't live in a real world. However, as with all characters, you must know the world you are writing about, and the story must be credible, so make sure that you plan your fantasy world carefully. Make plenty of notes on the characters, setting and any background information. Draw a map, if necessary, so you know where everything is situated. The same rules apply for science-fiction characters. Make sure you know the background of the planet they come from and that you make them credible.

Writing exercise

Choose a character from a modern children's book and write down at least five reasons why you think they are popular with children.

DEVELOPING CHARACTERS

The most important points when creating characters are to make them interesting, realistic and credible. Children have to believe in them enough to want to know what happens to them. The characters have to hold their interest long enough to entice them to read the whole book. To do this you need to know your readers and your characters really well. Here are a few tried and tested ways to get to know your characters:

1 *Writing a character profile.* Detail everything you can about your characters. Don't just write what they look like and their basic personality: think about how they walk, how they talk, the things they like such as their favourite song, colour and hobby. Think also of the things they hate. Is there anything they are scared of? Do they have any phobias? You won't need all this information in your story, but the more you know about your characters the easier you'll find it to write about them and the more credible they will seem to the reader.

2 *Having a conversation with your character.* There are several ways you can do this. A writer friend of mine told me that she signs into a private internet chatroom both as herself and her character, and then chats to them as if they were a friend. She assured me that it was an effective way to get

to know the character because it allows her to 'get inside the character's head' and really think about what they would do and say, and what their life is like. Alternatively, you can pretend that you're interviewing your character. Ask them lots of questions such as what they want most in life, what their worst fear is, and jot the answers down. You should then be able to form a profile of your character, which will be useful reference.

3 *Visualizing your character.* Draw a picture of your character or cut out a picture from a magazine of someone who is similar to your character. Pin this picture on the wall above your desk. Now think about the character. What is their name? How old are they? What do they like doing? What is their story? A picture can really bring a character alive for you.

4 *Keeping a diary for a week of your character's life.* Imagine yourself as your character and write the diary from their point of view. Think about what they would do, where they would go. Think also about the tone in which they would write the diary. This can be a very good way to get into your character's head and can really help you to write from their perspective.

5 *Thinking about how your character acts.* Put your character in a variety of situations such as falling out with a friend, playing the lead in a school play, feeling ill, being attracted to someone, witnessing a robbery. How would they act? What would they look like? How would their voice sound?

Writing exercise

Imagine you are your character's best friend, enemy, mum or teacher. What do they think about him or her? How would they describe the character to someone else? Write a profile from their perspective.

AVOIDING THE PITFALLS

+ If you base your character on someone in real life make sure that you tweak and add other characteristics, so that they aren't recognizable. If you don't, and the person doesn't like what you've written, you could be sued for libel.

+ Don't write a story using characters from existing books, television programmes or toys. These are copyrighted and you could be sued if you do.

+ Editors nowadays don't usually like stories about anthropomorphic animals. If your character is an animal then make that animal as realistic as possible, integrating its natural traits and characteristics. Don't just substitute an animal for a human character. If your character is a rabbit, let it live in a burrow; if it's a dog, show it wagging its tail, barking, sniffing around.

+ Never make a character perfect. Children don't want to read about a 'goody-goody' who never does anything wrong. They want to read about someone who messes up sometimes like they do; someone who gets scared or angry and is lonely or upset at times. So make your characters realistic and give them a couple of faults such as always being late or being a bit lazy.

Writing exercise

Create a character. Write down five things you know about them and five things you don't know.

CREATING A STORY AROUND YOUR CHARACTER

As I wrote earlier, the character always comes first for me. Once I've created a character I find it easier to think of a plot. There are several ways that a character can give you a story idea. Ask yourself these questions:

1   *What's your character's story?* Every character has a story. Their story is their life so far, their dreams, ambitions and fears. All of these factors can provide story ideas. Years ago, when I was writing for children's magazines, I had to come up with a variety of story ideas every week – not an easy task. Then, one of my editors gave me a tip I've never forgotten. She said, 'Give a character a problem and solve it.' I've often used this in my story plotting – adding 'in an unexpected way' to the end of her suggestion. Never end your story in a predictable way; you want to keep the reader guessing right to the end.

2   *What does your character fear most?* This is another reason why it's so helpful to do a character profile. You'll know what your character's strengths and weaknesses are, what they want most, what they fear, and you can build a storyline around that. For example, if a character is shy you could put them in a situation where they have to speak or act in front of a lot of people; if they are scared of heights you could create a situation where they are in danger and have to climb up somewhere to escape.

3   *What does your character want most?* Wish fulfilment is a good basis for a story. Simply think of what your character wants most but can't have, and then work out a story plot that makes this wish come true – but in an unexpected way, of course.

4   *What is your character's greatest strength?* If your character is a good singer then imagine them losing their voice or having a sore throat just before an important concert; if they are good at ballet or football imagine that they have twisted their ankle before a show or game. How would they feel? What would they do? How would they overcome it?

5   *How does your character react?* Put your character in a situation and think about how they would react to it. People react differently to the same situation. One of the exercises I often set my students is to create a situation, and then think about three different characters' reactions to it. For example, a dragon has injured its wing and is resting on a mountain. Now imagine someone finding him; a young trainee knight, a lonely little girl, a fairy or an inquisitive bear cub perhaps. Think about how each one would react and you'll see that you would have four completely different stories.

CREATING YOUR VILLAIN

You want your readers to be rooting for your Key Character and hoping your villain gets their comeuppance. So your villain needs to be a disagreeable sort of character such as a tell-tale, a sneak, a know-it all, a bully or a hypocrite. If the villain is unkind to your Key Character and tries to make trouble for them, they will instantly be disliked by your reader. Do remember, though, that whilst no one is completely good, they aren't completely bad either. So your villain needs some redeeming features. This could be something as simple as loving their pet toad.

> ### Top tip
> Your Key Character should have more good points than bad ones but your villain should have more bad points than good ones.

NAMING YOUR CHARACTERS

Character names are important. Names can give even inanimate objects a personality of their own. They help bring alive the characters in your story and help your reader form a mental picture of them. Would Thomas the Tank Engine be so popular if he was called Sid instead of Thomas? Does Harry Mouse have as much appeal as Mickey? And does Ron and Mabel sound as romantic as Romeo and Juliet?

So think carefully about your character's name and make sure it gives the effect you want. When children look at the blurb on the back of the book or open the first page and read the character's name, they immediately form an impression of that character and this could influence their decision whether to read the book or not. Think of the names of some popular children's book characters such as Artemis Fowl or Totally Lucy. If the authors had chosen names such as Albert, Florence or Cyril the characters wouldn't have sounded so appealing.

When I start thinking about the main character of my story, a suitable name often pops into my head. It's as if the characters introduce themselves to me. For example, the main character in my YA novel *Perfect Summer* is called Morgan and her friend is called Summer. Morgan is pretty and gutsy; Summer is beautiful and seems to have a perfect life (as the title suggests). It wouldn't have suited Morgan to be called Summer, or the other way around; from the moment I thought of the character, Morgan was her name. If I called her Anne or Judy, the story wouldn't have the same feel to it at all.

It's a bit of a different case for some characters, though, especially secondary characters. I often really have to think about names for these. If I'm stuck for a name I usually consider what sort of story I'm writing, and this will influence the sort of name I use. Characters in an historical story would probably be called Elizabeth, Victoria or Edward; characters in the pre- or early post-war period could be called Rita, Bert or Cyril; whereas characters in contemporary fiction would have more modern names such as Chloe or Ethan. A science-fiction or fantasy story would need more unusual names; for example, the main character in my sci-fi book *Cosmic Whizz Kid* is called Shiza, while the main characters in my fantasy novel *Firstborn* are called Myden and Tsela. Anyone reading the blurb on the back of these books will know that the characters aren't contemporary ones and will be prepared for a sci-fi or fantasy story.

Finding names

Stuck for a name for your character? Try these tips:

1 *Research.* Look at names in newspapers, magazines or the phone directory. For an unusual twist use a surname as a Christian name as I did when I chose Myden.

2 *Use the internet.* There are several websites that list baby names, often grouping them in different nationalities and explaining their meanings, too. An online search will provide you with a list of sites, but here are a few of the most popular ones:

www.mummypages.co.uk/baby-names – this site lists over 5,000 names from different nationalities.

www.thebabywebsite.com/babyNamesFinder.php – this site selects a name at random for you, as well as listing the most popular names. Select the 'Really Random Name' option if you want an unusual name.

www.rinkworks.com/namegen – this is a useful fantasy name generator, but be warned: some of them are really weird and comical!

donjon.bin.sh/scifi/name/#scifi_world – a sci-fi name generator.

3 *Be inventive.* You could always create your own name. J. M. Barrie, for example, made up the name Wendy when he wrote *Peter Pan.* Try mixing two names together such as Calum and David to create Cada, or Mary and Oliver to get Malo. Or simply change a letter or two so that Susan becomes Sukan or Andrew becomes Aldren. Don't make your names too hard to pronounce, though, as this can put off young readers.

4 *Use place or trade names.* These can be particularly useful for surnames. Trades such as Baker, Carpenter or Splicer all make good surnames, as do place names such as Ashby (from Ashby de la Zouch) or Moreton (from Moreton-in-Marsh).

5 *Naming your villain.* You might want to give your villain a suitably villainous name, as Lemony Snicket did with the nasty Count Olaf in his *Unfortunate Events* series.

> **Top tip**
>
> Check that your characters don't have similar-sounding names or names that begin with the same letter such as Ben, Beth, Billy and Belle.

SUMMING UP

+ Make sure that your character is realistic and one to which children will relate.

+ Get to know your character before you start writing your story.

+ Don't let your secondary or minor characters take the focus away from your main character.

+ Don't make your character perfect; give them some minor faults.

+ Choose your character's name carefully and make sure it suits them.

4

Pantsing or Plotting?

There are two main kinds of writers, *pantsers* and *plotters*. Pantsers 'write by the seat of their pants'; they get an idea for a story and just go with it, often not even knowing how the story will develop until they get to the end. Plotters plan everything in detail, often writing chapter outlines so they know exactly how they want the story to go.

I guess I waver between the two. I've always done a lot of commissioned work, which means the editor will want to see a synopsis and sometimes chapter breakdowns, so I've got into the habit of plotting to a certain extent, but I plot loosely to allow for the story to go in a different direction if necessary. Sometimes my characters can take over when I'm writing and ideas will come to me which I hadn't thought of before. There are strong supporters of both camps. I asked a few fellow authors whether they 'pantsed' or 'plotted', and here are their replies.

WRITING AS A PANTSER

There's nothing better than just sitting down and writing and seeing where it all leads. I very often work like this, particularly when starting something new. But I find that when I get well into writing the story there comes a time when I have to start plotting – even if only vaguely with random scenes. For me, it's a must or the story will end up moving too slowly. (Ann Evans)

Definitely a pantser. I do have an idea of my plot before I start, but it never ends up like I expected! (Jackie Marchant)

A pantser. I'm constantly surprised by 'what happens next' and love the feeling of not being in control. For me, it seems less contrived. I have no idea where I'm going – but always love it when I get there! (Wendy Meddour)

WRITING AS A PLOTTER

Whether a game story or a story, I plot or at the very least have a strong line thread. Keeps control. (Elizabeth Arnold)

I'm definitely a plotter. I couldn't write fiction at all until I started doing step outlines (a technique I've taken over from scriptwriting). All my attempts to just see where the characters would take me resulted in them all shrugging their shoulders in chapter 3 and going home. (Naff book this. Let's wait for something better to come along, etc.) I tend to decide on the end first and work back from there. (Diana Kimpton)

An attraction of planning for me is that it gives more scope for conscious craft, which I enjoy – I don't see how you can move around parts of a story, excising some, refining others and generally tailoring the whole to some overall purpose, unless you have a sense of that purpose and of the overall structure you're working with. (John Ward)

WRITING AS AN INBETWEENER

I began as a pantser and learned to plot. I feel it has done so much for my writing – I can now combine the two! (Leila Rasheed)

Not really a plotter or planner. I like to start with just an idea, and see what happens. After a page or two I sit and work out more about the characters, who they are, personalities and what they want/need. I usually have some kind of idea of what happens in the end but no real idea of how I am going to get there, but if I know the characters well enough and I am true to them; I love to let them take the lead and see what happens. (Linda Strachan)

I have a rough idea where I want the story to go. However, once I start writing the actual events seem to overtake me. I do not have an agent so I have only my publisher and myself to please, plus of course the current holder of the office of 'Jack the Station Cat'. (Alan Cliff)

THINKING BEFORE YOU WRITE

Everyone has their own way of working. However, I do think that plotting is the best way for a new writer because otherwise the story can tend to lack structure and focus. As you get more experienced then you will find the method that suits you best.

Whichever way you write you still need to know *who* and *what* your story is about. You should have at least a general idea of the plot, the main conflict and how it's going to be resolved. We've already discussed creating your characters so let's move on to building a plot.

WHAT IS A PLOT?

I mentioned earlier that I was given a tip at the beginning of my writing career to 'Give a character a problem and solve it.' This is excellent advice for coming up with a basic storyline. As E. M. Forster famously said: '*The King died. The Queen died. That is a fact. The King died then the Queen died of grief.* That is a plot.'

So the plot is something that has happened because of something else. For example, a boy is given a bike for his birthday then someone steals it so he tries to find out who is the thief. This could be the basis of a plot. Or you could turn the idea on its head and write the story from the point of view of the child who stole the bike. Why did they do it? Perhaps they needed to get somewhere very quickly and left the bike in a safe place for the owner to find? Perhaps they were following someone? Or trying to escape some bullies? Play around with your idea and see where it takes you.

DEVELOPING YOUR PLOT

To help you develop your story, ask yourself the following six questions:

1 *Who?* Who is your story about? Who is the main character, the person whose story you are telling? Who is the villain? Who are the other characters?

2 *What?* What is your story about? What is your character's main problem? What is stopping them from solving it? What happens?

3 *Why?* Why did it happen? Why can't your Key Character achieve their goal?

4 *Where?* Where is your story set? Where does your Key Character live? Does the action take place in a village, a city, a town, under the sea or in a fantasy world?

5 *When?* When does it all happen? Is your story a historical one? Set in the future? Work out a time sequence for your story. Does it take place over a week, a month, a year? Does the problem have to be resolved in a certain way?

6 *How?* How did the problem occur? How does it get resolved? How does your character succeed? How does the story end?

> **Top tip**
>
> If you're stuck for a plot, go back to the 'What if . . .?' question. What if your character lost their favourite toy, fell out with their best friend, had to move home, and so on?

USING THE SEVEN PLOTS

It's often quoted that there are only seven plots and that all books, films, etc. are a variation of these themes. Many people disagree with this and say there are at least twice that many, but I'm going to list the traditional seven as they might inspire you when you're stuck for an idea for a story. Obviously this list isn't set in stone and some stories are a combination of two or more of these.

1 *Rags to riches*. The tale of Cinderella is the obvious example of this plot but this theme doesn't have to mean that a poor person wins the lottery and suddenly becomes rich. Often the plot can be based around a character who is looked down on by everyone else, or feels inferior, the 'class nerd' for example, but throughout the story they are transformed and at the end they are happy with themselves.

2 *Tragedy*. *Romeo and Juliet* or *Othello* are the obvious stories that come to mind, but it doesn't have to be a love story. The traditional definition of a 'tragedy' is the downfall of the main character. A modern version of this theme is Linda Strachan's *Dead Boy Talking*, which begins 'In twenty-five minutes I will be dead.'

3   *Voyage and return.* This is where the main character goes off on a trip to a land or world far away, they face danger and have to go home. The film *E.T.* is an example of this, as is *Star Wars*.

4   *Quest.* As the name suggests, the main character has to go off on a quest to find someone or defeat something that is vital to save their world or someone's life. Philip Pullman's *His Dark Materials* trilogy and J. K. Rowling's Harry Potter series both spring to mind for this one. As does my ebook, *Firstborn*, a fantasy adventure story where two children have to find the Golden Dragon in order to save their world.

5   *Good versus evil.* This story plot involves the main character overcoming a monster – either a real monster or a big challenge. The tale of Little Red Riding Hood is the traditional example, but there are many modern books with this theme too, such as Maurice Sendak's *Where the Wild Things Are*, in which Max has to overcome his temper.

6   *Comedy.* For me, the *Just William* books are a good example of this. As a child, I used to laugh out loud whilst reading them. Modern examples are the *My Best Fiend* series by Sheila Lavelle and *Captain Underpants* by Dav Pilkey.

7   *Rebirth.* For this story plot the main character is 'reborn' in some way. Traditionally they are imprisoned or controlled by someone else and are then rescued – usually by a prince on a white charger in traditional fairy tales such as Rapunzel.

Writing exercise

Choose one of these seven plot ideas and write a story idea with this as a basis. Just write a paragraph to start with. Is your idea worth developing? Why not try this with all seven plot themes? Can you use any of your exercises as the basis for a story?

REALIZING THE IMPORTANCE OF CONFLICT

Conflict is the backbone of your story. Whatever your story is about, there must be some conflict that your character has to overcome. Conflict is what keeps your reader reading.

Think about the television 'soaps': there's always some drama in every episode. A character is having an affair, loses a job, is ill, gets divorced and so on. Some people complain about this and ask why the soaps are so full of tragedy and no one is ever happy. But if everyone had happy lives with no conflict in them the programme would soon get boring and no one would tune in to watch it. We keep tuning in to see what happens next, to see how our favourite characters will overcome their difficulties.

It's the same with books. There should be some conflict/problem that your main character has to overcome to hold your reader's interest. If everything is plain sailing then your story won't be an interesting read, so introduce the conflict as soon as you can. At first, this conflict should seem achievable, then throw obstacles in the way throughout the story so that it seems almost impossible for the main character to achieve their goal or overcome their problem. Keep your readers guessing right to the end.

FACING THE THREE MAJOR CONFLICTS

The conflict your character faces usually falls into three main groups:

1 *Conflict with other characters.* This is the most popular conflict used in books; think of the *Horrid Henry* books, where Henry and his brother Peter are always in conflict, or the countless books based around problems with the family or school friends/enemies. This is also popular with the older age group where the conflict is usually with parents, as in Rosie Rushton's *Just Don't Make a Scene, Mum!*

2 *Conflict with their own personality.* This is when your Key Character is faced with a situation where they have to struggle against their own nature. We talked about this a bit in the 'Creating a Story around Your Character' section of chapter 3. Many young children's books are based around this conflict, such as *How to Write Really Badly* by Anne Fine, which is based around Chester, who hates his new school, and Joe, who thinks he is no good at anything.

3 *Conflict with nature or circumstances.* This is often the basis of exciting adventure stories such as *Dolphin Song* by Lauren St John, but it can involve conflicts of birth or family circumstances over which your character has no control, such as being poor, from the wrong neighbourhood, too small, having ginger hair, needing glasses, etc.

USING IDEAS FOR CONFLICT

Here are some ideas for conflicts you could use in your story:

Other characters	Conflicts
Brothers/sisters	Argument
Friends	Feeling jealous
Enemies	Being bullied/feeling inferior
Parents	Not allowed to do something
Teachers	Not being good at a lesson
Step-parents	Feeling resentful
Grandparents	Come to live with Key Character's family
Neighbours	Grumpy/scary

Personality traits	Conflicts
Shy	Has no friends
Lonely	Has just started new school
Talks too much/stammers	Wants to be in a play
Scared of the dark	Has to go out late at night
Scared of heights	Friend lives on top floor of block of flats
Doesn't fit in	Wants to join the 'in' crowd
Can't swim	Is invited to a swimming party

Circumstances	Conflicts
Rain – flood	A trip has to be cancelled
Snow – avalanche	Trapped on a mountain
Sunny – drought	Trapped in a desert
Poor	Can't go to stage school
Too small	Can't reach things
Too big	Wants to be a jockey
Hair colour – red	Teased
Race/nationality	Bullied
Disability	Faces prejudice

Can you think of any other conflicts? Jot them down in your notebook or on the page here, if you don't mind writing on the book. Many writers add comments and notes directly on to their 'writing guide' books so that they don't forget them.

Writing exercise

Think of a character, then take a look at the conflict boxes above. Choose three conflicts for that character: one with other characters; one with their own personality; and one with their circumstances. Write a story plot for each conflict.

Top tip

You can increase the drama in your story by combining your conflicts. For example, your character could be stranded in a snowstorm with only two days' supply of food, or could start a new school only to discover that their worst enemy has moved to exactly the same school.

PILING UP THE CONFLICT

As you write your story it's a good idea to add minor conflicts to up the game and keep your reader hooked. Bring in other characters and plot developments to pile up the tension. Every time it seems like your character isn't going to succeed with their goal, bring in another complication, another hurdle for them to get over.

Writing exercise

Take a well-known fairy tale such as Puss in Boots or Cinderella and give it a twist. You could write the story from the point of view of one of the other characters as Philip Pullman did with I Was a Rat or tweak Sleeping Beauty so that it's a prince who falls into a deep sleep for a hundred years.

SUMMING UP

+ Whether you 'pants' or 'plot', you need to know what your story is about.

+ Every story needs some conflict in it.

+ Make sure your plot is suited to your target age group.

+ Pile on the conflict in your story to keep your reader interested.

+ Don't use well-worn plots; have an unusual twist.

5

Writing It Up

GET WRITING!

Writers write, it's as simple as that. If you want to write a story then you have to put pen to paper or fingers to keyboard. So once you have sorted out your story plot and characters, start writing your story down. You might find it difficult at first but there's no set word limit that you have to do every day. Start off with a couple of sentences, then as you get familiar with the story you'll find that you're writing more and more every day. And don't worry too much about writing in sequence; if a scene or conversation from later in your book comes to you – or even the ending – write it down. You can knock it all into shape later. The most important thing is to start writing.

WRITING IN YOUR OWN VOICE

Whenever I mention 'writing in your own voice' in my writing workshops someone asks me what I mean. It simply means that you should write in the style that comes naturally to you. Just as we all talk in a different way, we all write in a different way. You have a natural 'writing voice' just as you have a natural 'talking voice'. Think of well-known authors like Jacqueline Wilson and Jeremy Strong – they both have their own unique 'voice' that makes their work recognizable.

Note how established authors write and learn from them, but no matter how much you admire an author never try to copy them, because their voice is not your voice so your writing will sound stilted. An agent or editor is looking for your personal, unique voice. This is what will sell your work.

This doesn't mean that you should write however you want, disregarding story structure and never revising or rewriting. That's like saying speaking in your natural voice means that you don't have to bother about grammar, pronunciation or sentence structure. It simply means that you write in a style you feel comfortable with and tell the story in your own way.

DECIDING WHAT VIEWPOINT TO USE

Writing in the first or third person

There are two main viewpoints: the first and third person. Most children's books are told in the third person because it enables you, the writer, to get into the 'skin' of the Key Character and describe their thoughts and feelings. This viewpoint is best for beginner writers and for stories where there is a lot of descriptive narrative. If you use this viewpoint you must be careful not to let your own thoughts and opinions creep into the story. You should still only relate what the main character sees, hears, feels and knows.

Some writers prefer to use the first person viewpoint, thinking this makes a snappier read. It is true that readers can sometimes become more involved with stories told in the first person, and they can identify with the Key Character more, but there can be a tendency to just tell the story solely through the Key Character's thoughts instead of using action, description and dialogue. Also, the first person narrative can make it seem as if the character is standing on the sidelines, watching events, and is not really involved. However, when used correctly, the first person viewpoint can be very effective.

Here are two examples, one in the first person viewpoint:

The trouble with parents is they never discuss anything with you. They just decide and that's it. And today my parents decided to move my little sister, Gemma, out of their bedroom and into mine . . .

And one in the third:

It all started with the letter from the Ghost Council. 'Dear Esmeralda,' the black spidery scrawl said. 'In view of your reputation of being one of the most gruesome ghosts in England we would be honoured if you would give a speech at the Ball this year on the subject of Rules for Successful Haunting.'

'Just wait until that snooty Thora finds out!' Esmeralda thought as she read the letter for the umpteenth time.

As you can see, the tone of both stories is entirely different. Whatever viewpoint you use, keep to it throughout the story. You will confuse your reader if you mix the two viewpoints.

Writing from the multiple viewpoint

The multiple viewpoint is often used for more complex stories for older children, which are told through different characters' viewpoints such as Philip Pullman's *His Dark Materials* trilogy and Melvin Burgess's *Junk*. The story is told in either the first person or third person viewpoint but through the eyes of two or more characters. Usually each character is given a separate chapter but sometimes they are given separate scenes instead. Even if you use the third person viewpoint you should tell the story only from one character's point of view for each scene or chapter so you don't confuse the reader. Switching viewpoints in a scene is called 'head hopping' and is frowned upon by editors. Leave a space when you change a scene to another character's viewpoint so that the reader knows it's a change of scene/viewpoint.

Writing from the omniscient viewpoint

This is when the story is told as if from the outside, relating everything that happens. You are the storyteller and tell everyone's thoughts and actions. For example:

> It was early morning in the sleepy seaside town of Spindleton and the residents were all waking up. Lights were being turned on in the identical white houses that lined the narrow streets and kettles were being boiled.

This viewpoint used to be very popular some years ago but editors nowadays tend to prefer you to keep to the first person or third person viewpoint. One of the reasons for this is because an omniscient viewpoint means there is no Key Character to whom the readers can relate so they can feel distant from the story.

It can be used effectively to start a story, though, followed by a switch to the main character's viewpoint. For example, you could start with the above paragraph then carry on like this:

> Anna Turner at number 5 sat up in bed and yawned. She wished the holidays weren't over. She didn't want to go back to school. Little did she know that she wouldn't be going to school ever again. Today her life was about to change forever.

You could then continue the story in Anna's viewpoint.

Writing exercise

Write the first page of your story in the first person then the third person viewpoint. Which one did you find easier to write? Which one do you think sounds better?

Top tip

If you're struggling with your story, try writing it from another viewpoint. You might find it flows easier that way.

CHOOSING WHICH TENSE

Most children's stories are written in the past tense, recounting the story as if it has already happened, using 'he said' or 'she said'. However, some writers use the present tense to tell the story as it's happening, e.g. 'I rub my eyes and stare in disbelief.' They believe that it makes the story more immediate, especially for picture books. It can also work for longer fiction, as David Calcutt did in *Crowboy*:

So I'm outside the city one evening, on me usual rounds, sorting through the leftovers and picking me way through the day's dead. Not that there's much to be took. The best of the fighting's over now.

I wouldn't recommend a new writer using the present tense for longer fiction as it can be tempting to slip into the authorial voice. Whichever tense you use, be consistent throughout your story: don't swap halfway through from past to present or vice versa.

SETTING THE SCENE

The setting is where your story takes place; the time and location where it all happens. Try to create a setting that draws the reader into your story and helps them imagine that they are there. Paint the scene for them with careful use of adjectives and adverbs but don't get too carried away with description. Remember that the story is the important thing and the setting is the backdrop to your characters.

If you're telling a story set in the past, the future or on another world or planet, make this clear right at the beginning so that your readers know what to expect, otherwise they will presume that the story is happening in the present time.

The atmosphere is the mood or tone of the story. Make sure that you let your readers know what sort of story it is right at the beginning so they can get in the right mood to read the story. Choose your words carefully to set the atmosphere so they stimulate your readers' emotions and help them join in the experience of the story, make them laugh out loud, feel a shiver of fear or a tremor of excitement.

Writing exercise

Imagine an old house in the middle of the wood. Write a paragraph about it, setting the scene for a horror story. Then write another paragraph about it, setting the scene for a story set in the future. Think carefully about the words you use to describe the setting and atmosphere.

SHOWING NOT TELLING

Always try to 'show' things happening by using action or dialogue rather than 'tell' with passages of narrative. This makes the story more interesting for your reader and brings the characters alive. Rather than *telling* the reader that 'Jade was angry when she read the letter', *show* Jade going red in the face, clenching her fists, stamping her feet, screwing up the letter and throwing it in the bin. To quote Mark Twain, 'Don't say the old lady screamed – bring her on and let her scream!'

Writing exercise

Describe the characters' actions in the sentences below. Think about the expressions on their faces, how they would talk, the tone of their voice, the words they would say and the actions they would make.

1 Faye was sad.

2 Leroy was fuming.

3 Scarlett looked embarrassed.

4 Juan was tired.

BRINGING ON THE CONFLICT

If there's no conflict, there's no story, it's as simple as that. So don't be satisfied with just one major problem in your story: increase the conflict so that it seems that your character has no hope of succeeding. Remember to choose obstacles that your character could realistically overcome, though, and don't pile on too much conflict – your reader needs some relief from the drama. It's a good idea to inject some humour too, and a couple of reflective passages where the Key Character ponders over what's happened and wonders whether they will ever achieve their goal. Think of your story as ebbing and flowing like the tide, rising with drama and conflict, then slowing down again with humour or reflection.

APPLYING THE RULE OF THREE

A good guide for conflict, and a favourite with picture-book writers, is to use the rule of three. Let your Key Character have three attempts at overcoming their conflict before succeeding on the third attempt, three foes to face before reaching their destination, or three talismans to find before succeeding in their quest. This is a well-used ploy of storytellers; think of the Three Little Pigs and how the wolf has three attempts to blow the house down.

USING FLASHBACKS

Personally, I recommend that you avoid using flashbacks unless they are necessary to explain the character's motives or actions in the present time, or something of vital importance in the plot.

This is because when you use a flashback you are relating an event that's already happened and children want to know what's happening *now*, not what happened in the past.

If you feel that a flashback is necessary then make it clear when it starts and ends, without interrupting the natural flow of the story. Introduce the flashback by changing to the past perfect tense (inserting 'had' before verbs, also known as the pluperfect tense) as move you into it. If it's a short flashback then write it all in this tense, reverting to the normal past tense when the flashback has finished. For example:

> Aaleyah took the shell out of her basket and held it in the palm of her hand. Running her fingers over it she thought back to the day, two weeks ago, when she'd found it on the beach.
>
> She had been walking along, deep in thought, when she'd spotted it, shimmering in the sand. The rainbow colours had been so unusual that she'd picked it up right away. As she'd held it up to the sun and watched it shimmer and sparkle, she had known with absolute certainty that it was magic.

If it's a long flashback you can revert to the simple past tense in the middle of it and then back to the past perfect to end it.

USING PROLOGUES AND EPILOGUES

A prologue is an introduction at the beginning of the book to give the reader some information necessary to the story. It might give information about the characters, a backstory or the setting and is often set in the past. In my YA book, *Perfect Summer*, I used a prologue to set the scene and introduce a bit of mystery and tension to the story. My prologue is written in an omniscient viewpoint whereas the rest of the story is in the first person. This is how my prologue begins:

> They were on their fourth game of poker. The air was tense, they played in silence, speaking only when they had to.
>
> The burly man glanced at the five cards in his hand, his expression unreadable. 'I'll see you.' He took a drag of his cigarette and waited.
>
> The woman sitting next to him studied her hand of cards and sighed. 'I'm folding.' She placed the cards face down on the table, crossed her arms and sat back in her chair.

The prologue takes up a whole page. If you turn to the 'Bringing Your Characters on Stage' section of chapter 7, where I've related the beginning of the story, you will see that it is completely different to the prologue. The characters in the prologue play a vital part in the plot and will appear in the story again later.

An epilogue is like a prologue in reverse. It brings a conclusion to the story and is often set in the future. It can be useful if you are writing a sequel to your story as it can hint at an unsolved problem that will continue in the next book, thus whetting the reader's appetite. Epilogues usually start with something like 'Ten years later . . .'

Both prologues and epilogues are usually written in italics.

> ### Top tip
>
> Keep prologues and epilogues brief and concise. If you make them too long they may seem like a separate story.

SUMMING UP

+ Never copy another author, no matter how much you admire their work. Write in your own style and voice.

+ Choose the viewpoint you feel most comfortable working with and keep to it throughout your story.

+ Set the scene right at the beginning so that your reader knows what sort of story to expect.

+ Make sure there is plenty of drama and conflict to keep your reader hooked.

+ If you use a flashback make it clear where it begins and ends.

6

Letting Your Characters
Do the Talking

Children love dialogue; it brings the characters alive for them
and looks more interesting on the page than chunks of narrative.
Dialogue gives the characters personality and substance, which
makes them real to the reader.

MAKING YOUR CHARACTERS TALK

Your characters are all different and this should be reflected in
their speech. Think about the people you know and the different
ways they speak – not just their tone of voice but the words they
say and how they pronounce things. When someone you know
phones you, or you hear their voice outside, you can usually tell
who it is by the way they speak.

Years ago, when I was writing comic strips for children's magazines, an editor told me that the readers should know which
character was talking by what they said even if they weren't
identified in the text. Of course, I was writing stories around
well-known characters such as Winnie the Pooh and Tigger,
characters that each had a distinctive voice, and as there was a
limited word count (about twenty-four words) for each speech

bubble we needed to save words. But it was sound advice. Dialogue is what helps personalize and identify the characters: each character should have their own distinct voice.

Another way to help distinguish between your characters is to give them their own 'speech tag', something they often say, that is their 'trademark'. How many people do you know who have a favourite word or phrase that they repeat, or who constantly pronounce a particular word wrong? If you did this with a couple of your main characters it would help your reader identify with them more easily.

WRITING REALISTIC DIALOGUE

Dialogue should sound realistic but it shouldn't be written exactly as people speak in real life. If you listen to people talking they will often 'um' and 'ah' and say 'you know' or 'I mean' several times in a speech, but if you write your dialogue this way it won't look right. Written dialogue needs to be tighter than spoken dialogue.

Remember that children don't speak the same as adults, so don't make your characters talk like you do. Listen to how children speak, keep an ear out for the sort of words and phrases they use, and then inject them in your character's dialogue. But be careful not to use too much slang as this dates quickly; instead, use colloquialisms, contractions and sentence structure to show that a child is speaking. Colloquialisms and slang should only be used within speech marks, and don't use swear words in fiction for children under twelve.

Writing exercise

Write a conversation between a seven-year-old child and their parent, and then a teenager and their parent. Think about the dialogue, sentence structure and tone each would use.

Top tip

A good way to test if your dialogue sounds natural is to read it aloud.

USING DIALECTS AND FOREIGN LANGUAGES

Some of the characters in your book might be foreign or speak with a dialect. Obviously you need to indicate this in their speech, but don't overdo it as it will confuse the child reading the story. Use a familiar foreign word that children will understand such as 'Si' or 'Merci' then simply alter the sentence structure a little. You could write, 'I am being hungry', instead of 'I am hungry', for example, or 'Today I to the shop went.' This will indicate that English isn't the first language of your speaker.

If one of your characters is American then you could use the US spelling of words in that character's dialogue to reinforce the characterization. For example, if your character is of UK origin you would write, 'That's my mum.' If the character is American you would write, 'That's my mom.' Some words are different in America too, for example, 'pants' means 'trousers' and it's a 'garbage bin' not a dustbin.

Remember cultural differences too. Just as we notice that people do things differently or don't have the same sort of environment as we do when we go abroad, people from other countries notice this about the UK. So do your research and drop little things in a conversation to show that your character is of foreign origin.

USING DIALOGUE EFFECTIVELY

Never use dialogue just for the sake of it. When your characters speak, it must be for a reason and it must move the story along. Clever use of dialogue can impart lots of information to your reader in a far more interesting way than a block of narrative. You can use dialogue to do the following things:

Setting the scene

You can use dialogue to set the scene or give important information about time, place and setting rather than slow down the story with chunks of narrative. For example:

'My feet ache. We've been walking around this wood all afternoon.' Hal stopped and looked around. 'I told you there was no such thing as a marshmallow tree!'

Giving plot information

You can tell the reader something about one of the characters, a development in the plot or any information they might need to know.

'Listen! What kind of bird is that?' Myden asked, looking around. 'It's such a sad song.'

'It sounds like a phoenix,' Tsela said. She pointed over to the mountain. 'See, there it is!' (From my novel *Firstborn*)

Showing a character's emotional mood

Dialogue can be a very effective tool for increasing the drama and suspense in a story, for letting the reader know the character's mood or for adding humour.

'I'm going to look for Josh. I can't just sit here and do nothing. I've got to find him. I've a week's leave due to me so I'm taking that.' He ran a trembling hand through his hair, glanced at Mum then looked quickly away again. 'I'm sorry, but I've got to do this. I'll keep in touch.' (From my novel *Perfect Summer*)

Introducing a new development

A character's dialogue can be used to let the reader know of a new development, or that something is about to happen:

'The moon's turning blue,' Raheed's eyes were saucers of astonishment. 'And look, it's rotating!'

Building up tension

You can use a character's dialogue to let the reader know that something's gone wrong, thus adding tension to your story. Take a look at this extract from *Perfect Summer*:

'We've got trouble,' Summer announced, looking over her shoulder.

Jamie and I both followed her gaze and saw two LEF cars speeding towards us. They screeched to a halt and four officers spilled out.

'Don't move!' one of them shouted. 'You're all under arrest.'

FOLLOWING THE GOLDEN RULES FOR DIALOGUE

The first and most important rule is that dialogue must sound natural, but there are other things you need to think about when using dialogue:

+ *Make it clear who's talking.* This doesn't mean that you have to name the character and use an attribution word (such as 'said' every time), especially if there is an ongoing conversation between two characters. But do make sure that you repeat the characters' names now and again so that your reader doesn't lose track.

+ *Don't let one character speak for too long.* Dialogue, like spoken speech, is best kept short, so don't let a character ramble on and on. That would be as boring as listening to someone drone on in real life. If it's necessary for one of your characters to have a long conversation then interrupt it with a bit of action, such as them fidgeting, sipping from a drink or coughing. Or let one of the other characters interrupt the dialogue by asking a question, agreeing or simply nodding their head.

+ *Don't use too many attribution words.* Many new writers think that it's best to vary the verbs of speech so use as many different words as they can instead of 'said'. Their dialogue is littered with verbs such as laughed, gasped, exclaimed, whispered and guffawed. Whilst there are times when you will want to use another verb, make sure that it's for a purpose; otherwise keep to 'said'. Although 'said' might seem boring to you, the writer, the reader hardly notices so it makes the dialogue flow more smoothly. Never use smiled, laughed or grinned as an attribution word as you can't smile, laugh or grin words. Instead, write 'he said with a smile' or 'she said, smiling'.

+ *Keep adverbs to a minimum.* If you feel you need an adverb then see if you can think of a stronger verb instead. For example, instead of writing 'she said quietly', you could write 'she whispered'.

Also remember to always use speech marks, to put the final punctuation marks inside the closing speech marks and to start a new paragraph when someone different speaks.

Remember that children rarely stand still when they talk so show your character fidgeting about, twiddling with their hair and so on.

There are times when you'll want your characters to think rather than talk. This can be especially effective for scenes with only the Key Character in them, or to show the character's feelings. Remember to write these thoughts as if the character is speaking but don't use speech marks. For example: I wish she would shut up, thought Sam. All she ever does is moan at me.

Writing exercise

Rewrite this passage, taking out some of the adverbs and omitting or changing some of the attribution words.

> 'What do you think you're doing?' Susie shouted loudly, pointing to the yellow tee shirt that her sister was wearing. 'That's my best top.'
>
> 'I was only borrowing it,' Rachel exclaimed beseechingly. 'I'll give it you back.'
>
> 'But you'll ruin it,' Susie declared screechingly. 'You got coke all over my best dress last time.' She grabbed the hem of the tee shirt. 'Take it off, NOW!' she ordered, angrily.
>
> 'No, I won't!' Rachel retorted, fuming. 'You're just being mean. You've got lots of clothes. Why can't you share them?'
>
> 'Share them!' Susie repeated hysterically. 'I like that! You're always wearing my clothes but I can never wear yours.'
>
> 'Yes you can,' Rachel replied sneeringly. 'You can wear this.' She took a black dress out of her wardrobe.
>
> 'I don't want that. I want my yellow one back,' Susie begged sadly.
>
> 'Well, you're not having it,' yelled Rachel, defiantly. And she ran out of the room.

Do you think it sounds better now that you've edited it?

> **Top tip**
>
> A general rule is that children's books should be at least a third dialogue.

USING DIRECT OR INDIRECT SPEECH

Direct speech is when the character is actually talking, e.g. 'OMG! Look, something's in the garden!' Sonia shouted. 'It's moving! It's coming towards us!'

Indirect speech is when you report what a character has said. If we use the same example as above we might write 'Sonia shouted that there was a figure in the garden, and it was coming their way.' As you can see, direct speech can be far more effective. Use direct speech as much as possible as children find it more interesting, it brings the character to life and adds pace to the story.

When to use indirect speech

1   When you need to recap information that the reader already knows, e.g. 'He told her where he'd found the dragon egg.'

2   When one of the characters has to tell another character some information that you don't need to explain in full, e.g. 'She translated the letter for him.'

3   When relating a conversation about which the reader doesn't need details, e.g. 'She stood chatting to Mrs Barnes for a few minutes before setting off home.'

SUMMING UP

+ Don't keep varying your verbs of speech. Use 'said' unless you really need a different verb for effect.

+ Don't let a character ramble on and on without a break.

+ Read your dialogue aloud to see if it sounds realistic.

+ Don't use too much modern slang as it goes out of date quickly.

+ Make sure your dialogue fits your character's personality. A snobby girl will normally talk differently to one from a rough end of town.

7

Beginning, Middle and Ending

BEGINNING

Do you find it difficult to begin writing your story? Do you stare at the empty page or blank screen wondering where to start? If so, you're not alone. This is a problem common to most writers. So here are a few tips you might find helpful.

Starting with dialogue

This can be a good way to introduce your character or a problem, or to inform the reader of a few necessary facts. Take a look at this beginning from *Fishing for Clues* by Ann Evans:

> 'If we're going to bump into a dead body on this boat,' Candy Everton announced, following her dad and younger brother, Jake, along the canal towpath, 'I'm not getting on it.'

Jumping straight in with a dramatic scene or statement

This draws your reader into the story right away. Just a sentence can be effective for this. I used this type of beginning for *Dognapped!*, the first in the Amy Carter series:

I knew that dog was going to be trouble as soon as I saw her . . .

Starting just before an important change in the Key Character's life

This can whet your reader's appetite and make them want to read on to see what happens next. An example of this is the beginning of *Firstborn*:

The dragon swished her tail and snorted, sparks erupting from her nostrils. She turned to stare at Myden as he approached, her red reptilian eyes like flames of fire, the black slit of the pupils barely visible. As her gaze met his, Myden felt himself being drawn into the flame, down into the dragon's mind, so that he could almost taste her fear. What had terrified her like this?

Starting in the middle of a scene

Something is happening. Now! This is the beginning I used for *Smugglers*, the third in the Amy Carter series:

There it was again. I frowned at the distant flashing light, just visible over the rooftops from my attic bedroom. I'd been up late, talking to my buddies back home in the USA and had glanced out of the window before getting into bed. That's when I'd noticed the light.

Bringing your characters on stage

It's your Key Character's story so make sure you introduce them to your readers straightaway; don't leave them in any doubt whom your story is about. Many new writers do this by telling the reader all about their character. They start off by saying something like:

> Millie is nine years old. She had long black hair, green eyes and a turned up nose. She lived in a little cottage with her mum and Grandma down a country lane. Her favourite colour was green and her favourite food was chocolate. Her best friend, Sarah, lived around the corner . . .

This is all very boring. Don't 'tell' your reader all about your character; 'show' them by starting with your character in action, thinking, talking, doing something. For example, this is how I've introduced Morgan, the Key Character in *Perfect Summer*:

> '23.8!' I whooped as the score blazed on the wall for everyone to see. So far I was the top player.
>
> 'That's great.' Summer flashed me a too-bright smile. 'Let's see how I do.'
>
> Tucking her long blonde hair behind her ears, she pressed the silver button on the screen. A black ball rolled out of the chute. She bounced it against the wall like an expert.
>
> Tap, tap, tap.
>
> The two megafit lads who'd been watching nudged each other and moved a bit closer. Tall, slim, spike-gelled hair, looks to die for, the sort of lads Summer always attracted and I didn't. But then I wasn't effortlessly beautiful with creamy skin and diamond blue eyes like she was.
>
> 'Game commence!' the automated voice announced.
>
> Summer caught the ball as it bounced off the wall and

ran with it. A holoplayer flashed in front of her and she swerved just in time. If she touched a hologram she would lose vital points. The next holoplayer took her by surprise. She didn't stop in time and a buzzer sounded as she ran right through him.

'Penalty!' the automated voice announced.

Summer grimaced. Two penalties and she'd be out. I knew she was desperate to beat my score. Summer liked to be the best at everything, and she usually was. But I always beat her at Xball. That made me feel good even though I didn't actually like the game.

In this way I hope to let the reader know that Morgan is a bit envious of Summer who is prettier and cleverer than her. This story actually starts with a prologue, which I talked about in chapter 5.

The most important thing to remember is that you need to grab your reader's attention right away and hold it, so don't start your story with lots of narrative, explanation or backstory. Jump straight in and tell the tale; you can feed in any necessary background later. I often read a student's story and realize that it actually starts on chapter 2. They've spent the whole of the first chapter writing background information that might be useful for them to know but is boring for the reader.

Top tip

Take a look at the beginnings of some popular children's books. How do they draw the reader in? How effective are they? Would you begin the story the same way?

Writing exercise

Write the first page of a story using one of these opening lines.

1   *'Get down!' Mark yelled.*

2   *I couldn't believe my luck.*

3   *It was the scariest thing Zoe had ever seen.*

4   *Dan picked up the strange parcel and started
     unwrapping it.*

MIDDLE

Do you get stuck in the middle of your story, wondering what to write next? Many writers have this trouble and this is the part where the story can flag a bit. To keep your reader interested you need to keep them wondering what's going to happen to the Key Character. One way to do this is to bring in another conflict or introduce another character that can add some drama, humour or tension to the story. Another way is to take the story in an unexpected direction by having your Key Character getting lost, caught in a thunderstorm or snowed in.

I asked some children's authors what they did when they were stuck in the middle of the book. Here are some of their tips:

> I have tried lots of ways to get though this and usually it means I have lost faith with the story or the original idea. So I go back and read the original blurb I wrote for the story, the one that made me excited about writing it in the first place, or if it has veered away from the original

blurb I write another blurb. It helps focus on what/who is important. (Linda Strachan)

When I find myself struggling over what to write next, I know it's time to get away from the computer for a while and do something more 'manual'. Walking with the specific aim of solving the problem generally works for me. Very often, halfway around my usual route is when my thoughts start to take shape, and by the time I've reached home, I will often have the next sentences ready to be scribbled down or typed up. (Ann Evans)

Going for a run really helps as well. I once worked through a tricky plot point between miles 14 and 20 of the London Marathon, although that was an extreme case. (John Dougherty)

In fact, a lot of authors said that they found going for a run, doing housework or walking – with or without a dog – helpful for sorting out their thoughts and getting themselves 'unstuck'. So if you're stuck in the middle of your story, try leaving it and doing some 'mindless' task to give yourself space and time to mull it over.

Top tip

If you are really struggling with your story, ask yourself if you are writing from the right character's point of view. Is it really one of the other characters' stories?

Moving your story on

You can move your story forward in time by using a simple phrase such as 'later that day' or 'back home' or 'it was another week before ...'. Keep the phrase as simple and concise as possible and your reader will hardly notice it.

ENDING

This is where all the loose ends are tied up and the main conflict is resolved in a plausible but unexpected way. Increase the tension as you get near the ending to make it look like your Key Character will never solve their problem or overcome their hurdle. Give them a 'black moment' when it seems that they will fail. Then bring in the climax and suddenly, unexpectedly, they succeed.

Always make sure that the Key Character has developed in some way throughout the story. They must grow and learn something about themselves, someone else or life in general. Even if the problem hasn't been solved – perhaps your Key Character wants a puppy and can't because her sister is allergic to dogs – then the Key Character should have 'grown' through the story so that she can now deal with the situation and accept it, so it is no longer a major conflict for her.

Don't drag out the ending, giving pages of explanation. Stop when your story ends. When the main problem has been solved and all the loose ends have been tied up your story is over.

Always end on an uplifting note. This is a must for children's fiction, especially young children. For older children, not everything needs to end happily but the ending should be upbeat. There are some humorous books, such as those by Lemony Snicket, that have all sorts of disasters happening to the Key Characters and don't end on a happy note, but they are written in such a 'tongue-in-cheek' manner that the reader is entertained and knows not to take them seriously. This kind of humour is hard to do, though, so I suggest that beginners should avoid it and stick to the 'uplifting ending' rule.

Top tip

Never end your story with it all being a dream. This might have worked for *Alice's Adventures in Wonderland* but editors today don't like it. It leaves your reader feeling cheated.

Another way to end

Usually the story starts and ends with the Key Character. This can be a neat way of rounding everything up. But sometimes you might like to end with another character's thoughts, to emphasize the foreclosure of the story. For example, the main character in my story *Firstborn* is Myden, and although Myden resolves his conflict by the end of the story, the final paragraph ends with the Emperor's thoughts:

> Friends of the Emperor. Myden felt as if his heart was bursting with happiness. They had the Emperor's personal protection for the rest of their lives. It was amazing. So was all that stuff about the Shalram. Myden shook his

head, what did it matter, it was over now. He'd found his father and was going to live with him and Alrana. He had vowed never to return to Cryenia but things had changed. He had a family, a home and status now.

As he left the palace with Tsela, Indini, Tarka and Lawli, some other children came over to them.

'Do you want to play Dika Ball?' they asked.

'Good idea,' agreed Tsela. She turned to Myden. 'Do you want to be on my team?'

Myden looked at her smiling face then at the other children. 'All right.'

Back in the Palace the Emperor watched the children walking off together, their laughter echoing around the courtyard. Once he and Yandi had been like that. What had gone wrong? He passed his hand wearily over his eyes. What was the use of going over it yet again? Yandi was dead. His brother could harm them no more. Now, at last, he could marry and have a family himself. Cryenia was free.

Although it was Myden's story, I ended the story this way because the conflict was caused by a curse put on Cryenia by the Emperor's brother. This curse had cast a shadow over the Emperor's life and was now lifted. I felt that the Emperor acknowledging this gave final closure to the story.

Writing exercise

Write the last paragraph of your story. Are all the conflicts resolved? Have you ended it in an unexpected but credible way?

WRITING SEQUELS

If you're intending to write a sequel to your book you'll want to leave the ending open for a follow-on. This is best done with a hint that there are more adventures to come. For example, this is the ending of *Dognapped!*, the first book in *The Amy Carter Mysteries*:

> 'You're very clever . . . working out all of those clues,' Max said when I'd finished.
>
> 'I know,' I said smugly. 'Amy Carter, crime-buster – that's me.'
>
> I broke off two squares of the chocolate and popped them into my mouth. Maybe it wasn't going to be so boring in Little Cragg after all.

This ending shows that Amy has solved the mystery and gives a hint that there are more mysteries to come.

And here's the ending to *The Awakening*, the second book in the *Beast* trilogy by Ann Evans:

> Andrew slowed down to manoeuvre around another vehicle parked in the narrow bumpy lane. It was a roadworks lorry. Two men in yellow jackets were erecting a sign at the side of the road.
>
> Endrith Valley bypass. Work starts October for 26 weeks.
>
> Andrew waved as he steered past. 'That's going to cause a pretty big disruption when it starts,' he remarked.
>
> 'I wonder if it will disturb the ghost of Endrith Valley?' Beth asked, glancing at Daniel.
>
> An odd shiver ran through Daniel as he cuddled Scooby closer and murmured, 'I wouldn't be surprised.'

This hints that in the final book, *Rampage*, the ghost is awakened again.

CHOOSING A TITLE

The first and most important purpose of your title is to catch the reader's attention and make them want to read the book. The second purpose is to indicate what the book is about. So, it's worth taking time over your title and making sure that you get it right. Try to choose a short, snappy title that catches the reader's eye. If possible, avoid using 'A' or 'The' at the beginning of your title because there will be lots of other books with titles beginning like this on the bookshelf. You want your title to stand out from the rest.

Make sure that your title suits the content and theme of the story. You don't want children reading it to be disappointed, as they will be if they're expecting a horror story and get a magic one instead.

Don't worry too much if you can't think of a title before you write your story; just start writing and a title will probably come to you as the story develops. If not, then go back over the story and choose something from an event in the story. I chose my title, *Perfect Summer*, because Morgan thought her friend Summer had a perfect life and couldn't help envying her. As it turned out, Summer's life was far from perfect. However, for the three Amy Carter books – *Dognapped!*, *Sabotage!* and *Smugglers!* – I selected one-word titles that reflected what was happening in the story.

When choosing a title for your book, try to think of words that will intrigue children; 'magic', 'mystery', 'adventure', 'secret' and 'disaster' are all good words for strong titles.

Here are some titles of popular published children's books: *No-Bot, the Robot with No Bottom* (Sue Hendra); *Ketchup Clouds* (Annabel Pitcher); *Maggot Moon* (Sally Gardner). Do you think these titles are appealing to a child? What do you think the stories are about?

Top tip

The first thing a child usually does when choosing a book is to look at the title, then the cover, then flick open to the first page and read it. So make sure your title grabs their attention!

SUMMING UP

+ Grab your reader's attention right at the beginning of the book and hold it. Make them want to carry on reading.

+ If your book flags in the middle, bring in another conflict or character to liven it up.

+ Make sure all the conflicts are wrapped up at the end.

+ End on an upbeat note so your reader can close the book feeling content with how the story's panned out.

+ Choose your title with care. It's probably the first thing a child notices about your book.

8

Writing Chapter Books and Series

WRITING IN CHAPTERS

Once children have learnt to read they progress to 'chapter' books. These books tend to be popular as they are 'grown up' reading in bite-size chunks. To read a chapter isn't as daunting as to read a complete book so the child can read the story in stages.

Chapter books for five- to seven- year-olds have several small chapters, but for older readers the books have more words and the chapters are longer. Whatever the length, the same rule applies: the end of a chapter should be a page turner. The chapter should end with something happening that will make the reader eager to read the next chapter to find out what happens next.

If you're planning on writing a chapter book you might find it helpful to think of each chapter as a separate scene. Have something happen in it that moves the story forward such as a minor conflict thrust on the Key Character, a new discovery or an obstacle to overcome. Don't resolve this at the end of the chapter – keep up the suspense by carrying it on a little longer, leaving the reader eager to find out what happens next.

Writing the first chapter

The first chapter is the most important chapter. This is the one that will grab your reader's attention and set the scene for the whole book so you need to make sure that it gets off to a good start. You might need to spend a lot of time on this to get it right.

Let me use two of my own books, *The Gold Badge* and *Firstborn*, to illustrate this. *The Gold Badge* is a short chapter book for five- to six-year-olds and is about a young boy, Jack, who wants to win the gold badge that is awarded to one child in every class each week. There are five chapters in the book. The first chapter ends with Emily telling Jack she won the gold badge for smiling and being helpful:

> Well I can do that, Jack thought.
>   Next week he was going to win the gold badge. He'd make sure of it.

This will hopefully entice the child to read on to see if and how Jack succeeds.

Firstborn is a fantasy story for children aged nine plus. It is about two children, Myden, a poor landworker, and Tsela, the daughter of a Lord. They and all the other Firstborn children of Cryenia are captured by an enemy called the Isleck. Myden is the main character but some chapters are told from Tsela's viewpoint. Both children escape, helped by the dragons Bork and Jute, and are soon entangled in a dangerous quest to find the Golden Dragon and a battle so save Cryenia. In the first chapter, Myden notices that the two dragons guarding the city gates are restless, taking it in turns anxiously to fly off and scout around. Tsela comes to the Dragon Keep for the first time, saying she had a sudden urge to see the dragons. Then she discovers that she can talk to them. She tells Myden that the dragons told her that the Isleck are coming and they are terrified of them. The first chapter ends with Tsela's governess coming and marching Tsela way:

> Myden grinned as the woman – probably her governess – marched the girl off, ignoring her protests. Evidently even a Lord's daughter didn't always get her own way. Then he heard the swish of dragon wings and turned around to see Jute fly out over the city wall. So it was her turn to scout around now, to watch and wait whilst Bork rested in their cave. At least he knew what the dragons were waiting for. The Isleck.
>
> But who and what were they? And why were Bork and Jute so frightened of them?

Again, a child will want to read on to find out who the Isleck are and why the dragons are frightened of them. Hopefully, the friction between Myden and Tsela will also make the child want to find out more about them.

Writing a page-turner

A page-turner means simply that, i.e. something that makes the reader want to turn over the page and carry on reading. If you look at a selection of chapter books for younger children you'll see that chapters often end in the middle of a scene then continue in the next chapter. This is a device to hook the reader's interest and encourage them to carry on reading. Young children have a short attention span and will forget the thread of the story if it isn't continued immediately. If we take a look again at *The Gold Badge*, the second chapter starts with Jack smiling and trying to be helpful but things don't go as planned. The chapter ends like this:

> Jack was beginning to think that he wouldn't win the gold badge for helping after all.
>
> He was right. On Monday, Sara won the badge for writing a poem.

Every chapter deals with Jack's attempt to win the badge – and how these attempts backfire. Until finally, in the fifth chapter, he wins the coveted badge for helping a new boy settle into school.

As children get older and more fluent at reading, they can cope with more than one plot and more complex storylines. So books for eight-year-olds plus often end on one thing in one chapter then start the next chapter on something quite different, maybe even a totally different character. *Firstborn* does this. The first few chapters end dramatically, as in this ending for chapter 2:

> The night sky was lit up by dragon-fire as Bork and Jute battled to free the children. Snarling viciously, emitting green clouds of acid smoke that scorched across the darkness, the black dragons fought to keep their prey.
>
> Jute was beside them now. Myden heard the two dragons spitting and snarling at each other, felt the heat of their fire-breath on his face, smelt the whiff of sulphur in the air then a wave of nausea engulfed him as his captor ducked and dived to avoid Jute's attack. Suddenly the black dragon shrieked and lurched to one side as Jute attacked once more. Screeching in pain, it released its grip on Myden, sending him hurtling to the ground far below.

Later in the story Myden and Tsela get separated and one chapter ends with a dilemma for Myden but the next chapter continues with Tsela, and then ends with a dilemma for her. In this way I hope to keep up the suspense and encourage the child to continue reading.

Take a look at some of your favourite children's books and see how the chapters end, and then how the next chapter begins. Do you think the endings make the children want to turn the page to the next chapter? Would you have ended the chapters the same way?

The final chapter

This is the one where everything comes together and the problem is finally solved. Make sure that it's a plausible solution and that all the loose ends are tied up.

The Gold Badge ends with Jack finally winning the coveted badge for befriending a new boy, Gregory, and helping him with a project. *Firstborn* ends with Myden and Tsela defeating the Isleck and Myden returning to Cryenia to live with his father. There are a few twists also revealed in this chapter, which I won't give away here.

Writing exercise

Look at this list of genres below and for each one write a chapter ending that you think will entice children to want to read on. Don't worry about working out the plot – simply write a page-turner chapter ending.

1   A fantasy story.

2   A horror story.

3   A teenage romance.

4   A mystery story.

Top tip

Whatever the age group, the chapter must end on something that makes the reader want to keep on reading.

CHOOSING YOUR CHAPTER TITLES

Some chapters have titles, others are just numbered. If you choose to give each chapter a title – or are asked to by your agent/editor – then think carefully about them. Make sure that you don't give any of the plot away. For example, imagine your story is about a young girl, Eva, who desperately wants to win the swimming championships. She trains hard throughout the story, overcoming obstacle after obstacle. The reader is reading avidly, wondering what will happen next. Then they turn over the page to find a chapter titled 'Eva wins the medal'. How disappointing for the reader who now knows what's happened before reading the chapter.

The Amy Carter books are detective stories, so I tried to add to the intrigue by choosing cryptic titles. For example in *Dognapped!*, the first book in the series, Fluffy, the precious prize-winning dog owned by Amy's Gran, goes missing. I chose 'Fluffy' for the title of the first chapter and 'Missing' for the title of the second. This tells the reader that something has gone missing but not what it is. Later on in the book I use chapter titles such as 'A Lead' and 'A Sighting' as a sort of carrot to keep the reader hooked.

CONTROLLING CHAPTER LENGTHS

Chapters are often around the same length but this isn't essential; they can vary if necessary. Whilst I wouldn't recommend varying the length too much, don't be so obsessed about keeping to the same length that you drag a chapter out when it's come to a natural end or bring it to an abrupt halt when the scene isn't finished.

WRITING SERIES FICTION

Writing series-led fiction

You only have to take a look at the shelves in the children's section of your local bookstore to see the popularity of series fiction, sometimes with over twenty books in the series. Children love to read about more and more of the adventures of their favourite characters. Many popular series such as *The Secret Kingdom*, *Darke Academy*, *Dinosaur Cove* and *Animal Ark* are written by different authors and marketed under an 'umbrella name' that appears on the cover. These are called 'series-led' books and the idea is devised by the editorial team at the packagers (a company that creates books for publishers) who contact authors to 'put the flesh on the bones' of the story, which is then sold on to publishers. If you get asked to write for a series, remember there are two usual ways of working:

Writing for an already established series. The important thing here is to keep to the format and be consistent with characterization. Study a few books already published in the series to get the feel of the style, voice, characters and vocabulary used. Read, read and read. Don't start writing until you feel that you know the characters and the series format really well.

Writing for a new series. This is when the packager has an idea for a series and is looking for writers to write it up for them. Usually a few writers are approached, given details of the story and characters, and asked to write up a sample chapter each. You will probably be given a quite detailed plot, often also chapter breakdowns. The important thing here is to bring your own 'voice' to the series in order to breathe life into the characters in your own unique way. A writer or writers are then chosen for the series, which is sold on to a publisher.

Whether you are writing for a new or established series, you must be willing to collaborate and work closely with the editorial team, and to revise and rewrite your work as necessary.

The top two packagers in the UK are Hothouse publishing (www.hothousefiction.com) and Working Partners (www.workingpartnersltd.co.uk). I have worked for both of these packagers, writing the first book in the *Teacher's Pet* series for Working Partners and books three and four in *The Secret Kingdom* series for Hothouse. Sarah Hawkins, Senior Editor at Hothouse Fiction, said:

> We work with brilliant writers at all stages of their careers, from new writers who gain valuable experience from working with us (and often go on to have their own

books published), to established authors who enjoy writing something different under a pseudonym. We're always looking for people who are able to write to brief, but who will take our plot lines and add that bit of magic to really bring them to life.

The positives of working on series-led fiction are that you have a structure to work towards, you work collaboratively so have important editorial feedback, you get PLR (Public Lending Rights – see the Appendices), and if the series sells well it will look good on your CV.

The negatives are that as the books are usually published under one 'umbrella name', you won't see your name on the cover, you often have to work to very short deadlines, it can be high-pressured work, and you must be prepared to hone and rewrite according to editorial requirements.

Writing author-led series

Other series such as the popular *Horrid Henry* series are written by one author. If you are planning a series like this, then do make sure that your characters and setting are strong and varied enough to allow scope for a number of stories. Series often start off with four books, but then if they are popular will run on to six, ten or more. Each book in the series is a story in its own right, with a beginning, middle and end. Each book can be read alone without the other books in the series.

> **Top tip**
>
> A word of warning: publishing books is an expensive business so editors are often reluctant to take on a series by an unknown, untested author. I would recommend that if you have an idea for a series you write one strong 'standalone' book and send that, along with brief details of how it could be expanded into a series if necessary. That gives the editor the option of just publishing the one book at first, which isn't so costly.

THINGS TO CONSIDER WHEN WRITING YOUR SERIES

Are there any other similar series on the market?

No matter how good your series idea, if there is already a similar idea out there it's highly unlikely a publisher will be interested in yours. So do your research and make sure your idea is different in some way.

What's your audience?

Are you aiming at boys or girls or both? What age group are you trying to attract? These two things will affect the plots and vocabulary that you use.

Choosing one main character or multiple characters?

This is important because if there is only one main character in your stories then it has to be a very strong character with the potential for lots of different adventures/mishaps. Your series will probably be marketed under the name of this character – like *Horrid Henry* and *Mr Gum*. Of course, the character won't exist alone; like Horrid Henry, they will have a family, friends, neighbours and school friends who all provide the fodder for your Key Character's adventures, jokes or tricks. Where would Horrid Henry be without his brother, Perfect Peter? Even so, the character must be a realistic, credible one about whom children will enjoy reading. Although Horrid Henry doesn't seem a likeable character, it's his naughtiness that children love. I believe that one reason for the success of this series is that many of the avid readers would love to be just like Henry and revel in his misdeeds.

Choosing multiple characters for a series

Other series books, such as Linda Chapman's *Skating School*, are based around a school or another fixed setting. Often, as in *Skating School*, there is still one Key Character, but in other series each book tells a different character's story. Helena Pielichaty's *Girls FC* series is about a girl's football team, with each book featuring a different player as a main character and dealing with their personal issues as well as the progress of the team.

The most important thing to remember when writing a series is to be consistent with your characters and to have variety in your storylines. If someone hates grapes in book one, they should still hate grapes in book six unless you've explained why they've changed. And if you write story after story about your main character getting lost then someone rescuing them at the last minute, you'll soon lose your reader's interest – not that your idea is likely to find a home if it's so predictable!

> ### Top tip
>
> Keep a record – it's called a 'bible' in the trade – of all the important facts: names and descriptions of characters, the setting, birthdays, plots you've used and so on. That way you can easily check any facts you need to know.

WRITING TRILOGIES

A trilogy is a story told in three parts. Each story is connected, and whilst the books can be read alone, a main plot runs through the three books and isn't resolved until the end of the last book. For example, Ann Evans's *Beast* trilogy follows the adventures of Karbel, the ghost of a sabre-toothed tiger who has been haunting Endrith Valley in the Scottish Highlands for 10,000 years. The three books, *The Beast*, *The Reawakening* and *Rampage*, can be read as standalone stories but are linked by the theme of Karbel's spirit, which finally finds peace at the end of book three.

A trilogy often involves some sort of quest, usually based in a fantasy world, with lots of drama, sorcery and magic, and a variety of dark characters. *The Lord of the Rings* is an example of this, as is Philip Pullman's *His Dark Materials* and William Nicholson's *Wind on Fire* trilogy.

If you want to write a trilogy, I suggest that you loosely plan out all three stories, so that you can ensure the plot has enough depth and substance to run over three books, and write detailed notes about your characters and setting (as mentioned in the previous section on series). If you are struggling with the plot for the second or third book, ask yourself if your story should be one long 'standalone' book instead. If you have to pad it out, then don't write a trilogy.

SUMMING UP

+ End each chapter on a page turner.

+ Your chapters don't have to be the same length; end a chapter when the scene ends naturally.

+ Don't give away the plot with your chapter titles.

+ When writing for a series, remember to be consistent with characters and setting.

+ If you're planning a trilogy make sure that your plot and characters have enough scope for three books.

9

Writing Educational Fiction

The main difference between writing educational fiction and mainstream fiction is the vocabulary and grammar restrictions. Whilst this kind of writing isn't for everyone, it might be something that you're interested in.

RESEARCHING EDUCATIONAL PUBLISHERS

Many publishers have an educational division where they publish stories for use in the classroom either as part of a reading scheme or to supplement it. The most well-known reading scheme is the Oxford Reading Tree developed by Oxford University Press, but several other publishers such as HarperCollins, Usborne and Scholastic publish educational fiction and reading schemes. An internet search on 'educational publishers' should provide you with a list of publishers' websites you can browse. Take a look at the books listed on each website and, if this kind of writing appeals to you, see if you can get hold of a few for research. This can be difficult as reading schemes are usually sold in multiple packs, but if you have a young child at school, or a relative with a young child at school, you might be able to borrow a book or two.

APPROACHING THE PUBLISHERS

If you are already a published writer for children of a certain age, or a teacher familiar with reading schemes, you could write, enclosing a CV, to offer your services. If you haven't been published before, or write for a different age group but would like to write for a reading scheme, then it would probably be best to send a sample of your writing along with your query.

WRITING FOR EARLY READERS

If you are asked to write for a reading scheme you will probably be given a very detailed brief to keep to and a list of words that you can use. Reading schemes are divided into levels according to a child's reading age, which doesn't always match their chronological age. You'll be told the level for which your story is to be written and probably be asked to introduce a certain number of new words.

When I wrote my book *All Aboard!* for the Reading Heroes reading scheme (published by Parragon) I was given a selection of levels and topics from which to choose. Level 1 was for beginner readers; Level 2 for improving readers; Level 3 for confident readers (this was the level for which I was asked to write); and Level 4 for fluent readers.

Select the level you feel most comfortable writing for, study the brief carefully and adhere to it. Be prepared to change words and simplify sentences if the editor asks you to do this. Your story should be simple but entertaining. It isn't an easy task, and educational writers rarely achieve any kind of fame, but it's a worthwhile one as you'll be helping children improve their reading skills.

> **Top tip**
>
> Read a few books in the reading scheme for which you wish to write. They are more difficult to write than they seem. Telling an interesting story with a limited vocabulary isn't an easy task.

WRITING FOR THE NATIONAL CURRICULUM

Some educational fiction books are directly linked to the National Curriculum. If you go on to the website at www.education.gov. uk/schools/teachingandlearning/curriculum/primary you will find details of the subject matters for each area of learning. For example, in the criteria for teaching English for Key Stage 1 Literature it states:

The range should include:

a. stories and poems with familiar settings and those based on imaginary or fantasy worlds
b. stories, plays and poems by significant children's authors
c. retellings of traditional folk and fairy stories
d. stories and poems from a range of cultures
e. stories, plays and poems with patterned and predictable language
f. stories and poems that are challenging in terms of length or vocabulary
g. texts where the use of language benefits from being read aloud and reread.

Educational publishers are looking for stories that fit into these requirements. If you can think of an idea that meets these, such as writing a story based on an imaginary world or retelling a traditional folk story, then you'll have more chance of it being accepted for publication.

Linking stories or plays to the National Curriculum

If you browse through the National Curriculum website you'll see the criteria for other subjects such as history and geography. If one of these is your favourite subject you might like to write a story based on the period the curriculum covers. Stories with fictional characters but based on facts, for example, the life of a boy living in Roman Britain, are called 'faction'.

An example of writing for the National Curriculum

A few years ago I was commissioned to write a selection of twenty-seven plays for Hopscotch Educational titled *Quick and Easy Plays for Primary Schools*, to fit in with the National Curriculum. It was aimed at seven- to eight-year-olds. I had to write three plays for each topic and linking theme, which were all connected to the curriculum subjects. These are the topics and themes I was given:

Stories with Familiar Settings
Topic: Families. Linking theme: Moving house
Topic: School. Linking theme: Friends
Topic: The Optician. Linking theme: Taking care of eyes

Myths and Legends
Topic: Good over evil. Linking theme: Knights

Topic: Wise over foolish. Linking theme: Clever females
Topic: Weak over strong. Linking theme: Giants

Adventure Stories
Topic: Exploring new worlds. Linking theme: Into space
Topic: Evacuation. Linking theme: New experiences
Topic: The sea. Linking theme: Boat trips

I had to provide teachers' notes with each play, including costume and prop instructions. Quite a task!

WRITING HI-LO FICTION

These books are aimed at children – mainly boys – who are reluctant readers, but they are not the same as books in a reading scheme. Basically, the books are *high* in content and *low* in terms of reading ability. Children, especially boys, don't want to be seen reading 'babyish' books that are aimed at younger readers so the idea is to give them a proper book to read. The author is expected to write a gripping story with a limited vocabulary. Barrington Stoke (www.barringtonstoke.co.uk) leads the field in this kind of writing. A quick glance at its website shows titles such as *A Dinosaur Ate My Socks* by Eric Brown (reading age eight, interest age eight to twelve) and *Alien* by Tony Bradman (reading age seven, interest age teen).

Another publisher specializing in this field is Ransom Publishing (www.ransom.co.uk), which publishes several action-packed series as well as standalone titles. Anne Rooney's *Vampire Dawn* series for Ransom starts with an establishing volume in Hungary and then follows the stories of the different characters, dealing with the same situation (having been turned into a vampire) but in different locations once the characters leave Hungary. The books are all short (8,000 words each) and are for less confident readers aged fourteen plus. Anne says:

> The challenge of writing this type of book is that they have to be packed with interest and deal with plots, characters and themes that appeal to young adults – but the vocabulary and syntax have to be easy for readers to deal with. It needs as much story as a full-length novel, but compressed so that it's exciting and fast-paced. It's difficult, but enjoyable and immensely rewarding.

SUMMING UP

+ Research publishers' educational lists.

+ Write for the level with which you feel comfortable.

+ Keep your sentences short and the vocabulary simple.

+ Try to link your work to the National Curriculum.

+ Remember to make your story interesting – educational fiction shouldn't be boring!

10

Crafting the Synopsis and Proposal

Unless you are writing a picture book or short chapter book under about 4,000 words an editor will ask initially to see the first three chapters of your story and a synopsis. The purpose of the synopsis is to tell the editor what your story is about, and to show that your plot is a strong one and that you have resolved it satisfactorily. The purpose of the first three chapters is to whet the editor's appetite while introducing your characters and story, and you should reel them in enough to make them want to read more.

WRITING THE SYNOPSIS

Not many writers like doing a synopsis and new writers in particular get rather worried about the idea. When I write a synopsis I usually write it in the present tense to differentiate it from the actual story and to make the events seem more immediate, as if they are actually happening. I also use single line spacing.

The main things to remember when writing your synopsis are to:

+ *Tell the editor the title of your story, the genre and the age group it's aimed at.* I find that the best way to do this is to have the title as your header with the genre and age group in brackets underneath. For example, you could write in brackets, 'A mystery thriller for eight- to ten-year-olds'.

+ *Introduce your character at the beginning and make them sound as interesting as you can.* This doesn't mean that you should describe them in detail – simply something like, 'When ten-year-old Anton found a magic lamp he couldn't resist using it, even though he was warned not to.'

+ *Let the editor know what the story is about and where it is set.* The editor will want to know the main plot and where the action takes place.

+ *Bring in your main conflict/problem as soon as possible.* Let the editor know what the main conflict is and briefly mention the other major conflicts. For example, 'Anton's problem got worse when ...'

+ *Let the editor know how the story ends.* Don't tease the editor by making statements such as 'Will Anton ever get home again?'

It can be a good idea to write a synopsis once you have worked out your storyline to give you some sort of structure to which to work and to keep your story on track. Remember that the purpose of this synopsis is to allow you to plan out the main events of your story. It is not cast in iron. You can alter it as you go along if necessary. It is merely a basic plan to aid you when you are writing.

If an editor commissions you to finish your book on the basis of the three chapters and synopsis you have submitted, they will expect you basically to keep to the synopsis but won't mind if you make minor changes if you think it improves the story.

A sample synopsis

Here is the synopsis I wrote for *Perfect Summer*:

> Growing up in a society so obsessed with perfection that the government gives people grants for plastic surgery, Morgan can't help being a bit envious of her best friend Summer. Summer is beautiful and rich, her father is a top plastic surgeon and her mother is a beauty consultant with a celebrity client list. Her life seems so effortlessly perfect. Whereas Morgan isn't so rich or beautiful and her little brother, Josh, has Down's syndrome – which, according to the Ministry and society in general, is a crime. Morgan's parents defy pressure to put Josh in a RLC (Residential Learning Centre) where all 'damaged' children and adults are sent, and he is a much-loved part of the family. Then, one day, Josh goes missing.
>
> Once the police learn Josh has Down's syndrome they lose interest, as does the media. So Morgan decides it's up to her to find her brother. She trails the internet and discovers a website by a boy, Jamie, whose disabled sister, Holly, was kidnapped two months ago. She contacts Jamie, and learns that so far thirty disabled children have gone missing that year. They join forces and, helped by Summer, try to find the missing children.
>
> The Ministry warns them off when they try to draw the public's attention to the missing children, and when

they hack into Summer's dad's computer system for more information, Summer is banned from seeing Morgan. Jamie and Morgan try to prevent a young girl, Emma, from being kidnapped and end up getting kidnapped themselves. They are taken to a research centre where they discover that a top scientist and a ruthless gang are behind the kidnappings, killing the victims and selling their organs to surgeons who don't ask where they come from. Jamie is heartbroken to discover his sister has been killed.

Morgan and Jamie manage to phone Summer to let her know what's happening. When they discover links to the kidnappers and the hospital where Summer's surgeon father works, Morgan fears that he's involved. They escape and find Emma and Josh but there is no sign of Holly or the other missing children. They bravely fight off the kidnappers and drive off in the kidnappers' car, but are pursued and overpowered. Just as they think this is the end of the road for them a fleet of police cars pulls up. Summer has alerted the police. To Morgan's amazement, Summer's dad is with the police and runs to Emma, hugging her. She is his daughter from an affair he had several years ago.

Summer and her mother are devastated and decide to move out of the area. Morgan sadly watches Summer walk away, knowing that her friend's 'perfect life' has been shattered and that she will miss her friendship. She is so glad her little brother is alive and that she still has Jamie's friendship and resolves to never get hung up on 'perfect looks' again.

> **Top tip**
>
> Keep your synopsis as short and concise as possible. Don't bore the editor by detailing every scene. Just mention the important ones.

I asked some fellow authors to share their tips on writing a synopsis and this is what they said:

Force yourself to keep it to a single side of A4. No book is so long that it needs more than that. (Nick Catman)

My advice would be to follow through the protagonist's experience of events in a clear, logical way. Saying for each key stage of the story what happens, why, how the main character responds and what this then leads to. (Sandra Glover)

Many writers hate writing a synopsis because it reduces their beautiful book to two (the usual maximum in the absence of stated wishes by the agent/editor) stark pages. But it is actually a useful writing tool and, treated as such, becomes less worrying. Written in advance, it can help you focus on the core of your book, show you a path to follow (even if you end up straying), or flag up flaws that you need to know about. Written after the book, it shows the agent or editor that the book works as a rounded whole. And it's much easier than you think! (Nicola Morgan, author of *Write a Great Synopsis*)

Writing exercise

Choose a short book that you enjoy reading and write a one-page synopsis of it, using the present tense. Remember to mention the main plot, the major conflicts and how they are resolved, and how the book ends.

WRITING THE FIRST THREE CHAPTERS

The first three chapters are vital for attracting the editor's interest. By the end of the first chapter it should be obvious what conflict or problem your Key Character faces. By the end of the second chapter it should seem clear that the Key Character is going to have difficulty overcoming this problem or conflict, and by the end of the third chapter the conflict should have increased considerably.

If we take a look at my book *Perfect Summer*, the first chapter introduces Morgan, her world, her prettier, richer friend Summer, and the pressure the police put on her parents to put her disabled little brother, Josh, into a home. In the second chapter we are shown how different Summer's affluent and carefree life is to that of Morgan, Josh goes missing and we learn that several other children with disabilities have gone missing over the previous three months. In the third chapter the pressure is increased by her parents arguing and her dad storming out, the police calling off the search for Josh, and Morgan deciding to try and find her little brother herself.

As you can see, I've upped the stakes as the book progresses.

FIRST PAGE CHECKLIST

The first page of your story is the most important page of all. This is the page where you need to grab your reader's attention and make them want to read on. As I mentioned earlier, a child will often look at the cover of a book, read the blurb on the back, and then turn to the first page and read a few lines before deciding whether to buy it or not. So go back over your first page and check that:

1 *You've grabbed your reader's interest right away.* If you don't, you will lose the reader. A child will glance at the opening paragraph of a book and, if it doesn't appeal, probably won't read any further. So don't waste words describing the sunset. Grab their attention – and hold it.

2 *You've introduced the Key Character.* Within the first couple of sentences you must tell your reader who the Key Character is, making sure you name them, and something about their personality that will instantly attract the reader's sympathy. Your reader wants to know who the story is about and what sort of person they are.

3 *You've set the scene.* Where does your story take place? At home, at school, on a farm, in space? What time of year is it? Is it a weekday, a weekend, a school holiday? Let your reader know as soon as possible so they can place the character in a setting.

4 *You've introduced the problem.* What is the purpose of the story? What is the character trying to achieve or overcome? Make sure that your reader knows this so they can identify

and sympathize with the main character. If a character doesn't have a problem to solve then you don't have a story.

5   *You've set the mood.* What sort of story is it – funny, adventure, scary? This should be clear in the opening paragraph then your reader will know what to expect from your story and get in the right mood to read it.

6   *You've hinted at the conflict.* What is stopping the main character solving their problem? Make sure that the reader is aware of the conflict and the consequences of it not being resolved.

7   *You've hinted at the solution.* At the beginning, the problem shouldn't seem insurmountable, just difficult. It is only as the story develops and the Key Character faces other obstacles that the problem should seem to be insurmountable.

WRITING A PROPOSAL

If you're planning a trilogy or a series of books then it's best to write a proposal to outline your basic idea, the characters and how future books will develop. The proposal should consist of the following:

+   A title page.

+   A summary of the series idea.

+   A list of characters.

+   Profiles for the main characters.

+   The setting/background.

+ Story outlines for the first four stories.

+ A synopsis and the first three chapters of the first story in the series.

Let's take a closer look at these.

Arranging the title page

This should state the name of the series and a simple sentence saying what the series is about; for example, 'An exciting space adventure series for six- to eight-year-olds.'

Giving a summary of the series idea

Try to think of a catchy short sentence that describes your series idea and will grab the editor's attention. Something like, 'When Elena is asked to help the fairies defeat the Wood Ogres she finds herself caught up in a world of magic and adventure.'

Listing the characters

There will be some regular characters that appear in every series so let the editor know who they are.

Profiling the main characters

If your series is about the various adventures of a set of characters, two girls perhaps or a sister and brother, the editor will want to see if they are the sort of characters children will want to read about over and over again, so write a character profile for them. This can be just a short paragraph, but detail their main character traits, anything that will endear them to the reader and any catchphrase or habits they have.

Describing the setting/background

You don't need to give too much information, just a couple of sentences to explain the setting and any necessary background information.

Detailing story outlines

The editor will want to know that your series has potential for several stories, and that you can come up with ideas for these. So, provide a paragraph or two outlining a possible plot for four stories. If you have ideas for more stories that this, then say so. Just a sentence on each one mentioning the main plot will be fine for these.

Providing a synopsis and three chapters

Write the first book in your series and send a synopsis and sample chapter of this along with the proposal. Linda Chapman, author of the popular *My Secret Unicorn* series, advises:

> When writing a series proposal I think one of the most important things is to help a commissioning editor reading the proposal really 'see' the book. Start the proposal with a catchy strap-line and then sum the series up in just a few lines. Pretty much all of the great series can be summed up in a sentence – their simplicity is part of their success. A good proposal should help an editor 'get' a series concept straight away. And it should seem professional. After the initial few lines specify what age group your series is for, how long the books will be and who your reader is going to be. After that you can then go into the story in more

depth, but remember a series is essentially a commercial book and you have to show that you have an awareness of the market. A good idea on its own is rarely enough!

> ### Top tip
>
> Make sure you write your first story in full before you send out your proposal. This is for two reasons: to make sure you can do it, and so that it's ready to send out if an editor asks for it.

SUMMING UP

+ Your synopsis is an overview of the story, not the complete plot.

+ Keep your synopsis to a maximum of two pages, preferably one.

+ Tell the editor how the story ends.

+ The first three chapters must tell enough to make the editor want to read on.

+ Sum up your basic idea in just one snappy sentence.

11

Submitting Your Work

You have only one chance to impress an editor or agent so never, every send your work out until you are sure it's the very best you can do.

REVISING AND REWRITING

Be prepared to revise and rewrite your work several times. I don't know any professional authors who submit the first draft of their work. They read it, revise it and rewrite it until they are satisfied that it is their best work before they submit it. Personally, I do several rewrites of my work, especially the earlier chapters as these are the ones where you are just getting into the flow of your story and are inclined to write too much information or not get the flow smooth enough. So don't skip this vital stage if you want to get your work published. I would recommend the following stages of revising.

Reading through the whole manuscript first

You'll find it helpful to read your story from beginning to end first. This will enable you to get the overall gist of it and check that it flows correctly. If you notice anything glaringly wrong then make a note of it but don't stop reading to alter it. Take your time, stopping for breaks whenever necessary, or putting it away to finish reading another day. Don't skim-read your book otherwise you will miss things you need to revise. When you've finished, ask yourself the following questions:

+ Are you satisfied with the overall impression?

+ Does the plot work?

+ Are the characters realistic and credible?

+ Is the ending credible but unexpected?

+ Does the story do what you set out to do?

+ Are there any obvious grammar, spelling or punctuation errors? Don't get too bogged down on this yet; correct any that you notice but concentrate mainly on the story itself.

Checking for inconsistencies

When you've altered the glaringly obvious errors you noted during your first overall read, go back and check for any inconsistencies. Things to look for are:

+ Are all the characters consistent? You would be amazed how many authors give their character blue eyes in chapter one and brown eyes in chapter six!

+ Is the setting consistent? You don't want your characters walking over a bridge to get to a village in one scene then the bridge suddenly disappearing in another scene when they leave the village – unless they leave by a different exit, in which case you should mention this.

+ Are all the subplots resolved? Make sure all your loose ends are tied up.

+ Is it obvious where any flashbacks start and end?

+ Does the time span work? Make a note of the days the story covers and make sure that the sequence is correct. If it's Tuesday in the story and your character is looking forward to something happening on a Friday, make sure you do your sums. Don't say in two days' time if it's three!

+ If you've used any magic or special powers in your story, are they consistent and credible? If a character has to tap their ear and say a spell three times for it to work, make sure they do so every time – unless they do it wrong and the spell doesn't work.

+ Have you got your facts right? If your story is set in the past, check and make sure that you are writing true to that time. Remember how everyone chuckles when an actor in a film set in Roman times wears a wristwatch? If your story is set in another country or a place to which you have never been, do your research. If you are writing science fiction then check that the science you have used makes sense. If you don't check your facts, you'll be found out. Even if your story gets past an editor, some clever child will spot it, believe me.

Checking the text chapter by chapter

Have another read through and make sure that you haven't missed anything. Ask yourself:

+ Is your dialogue realistic? Does it suit the personality of the character who is speaking? Have you used the correct attribution verb? Is it clear who is speaking?

+ Is your narrative effective? Does it describe the scene without being too wordy?

+ Does every scene add something to the story? No matter how clever you think a piece of dialogue is, or how beautifully you've described your setting, if it isn't necessary to the story delete it.

Checking the structure and flow

This is a very important stage so don't skip it. Read through your manuscript slowly and check the following:

+ Has it got structure to it? Is there a beginning, middle and end?

+ Is there enough – or too much – conflict?

+ Does it flow smoothly? Do any bits sound stilted or awkward? Read aloud any passages you aren't sure of and tweak them until you're satisfied with them.

+ Does the story go a bit stale in the middle? Do any parts of it ramble on a bit?

+ Are the sentences or paragraphs too long? This, of course, depends a lot on the age of the reader. Check that the length of the sentences and the vocabulary you use are suitable for the age of your reader. If you have some overlong paragraphs, break them up into shorter ones.

+ Have you used too many adjectives or adverbs? Remember that whilst adjectives and adverbs are useful tools to add colour and description to your story, they are often overused. An editor once told me that a good rule is no more than three adjectives or adverbs on a page. I'm not saying you have to stick religiously to this, but do restrict their use. See if you can replace them with a stronger verb or noun instead.

Checking your spelling, grammar and punctuation

When you are satisfied that your story is the best you can write it, go through and check your spelling, grammar and punctuation. Read your work slowly, checking it page by page. Check the following things:

+ Are there any typos or incorrect spellings? Your spell-checker, if enabled, should underline them in red for you, so go over your work carefully and check for the squiggly red lines.

+ Have you used the correct word? Your spell-checker won't tell you if you've used 'piece' instead of 'peace' or 'bare' instead of 'bear' – which could be an embarrassing mistake!

+ Have you used the correct punctuation? Is your dialogue enclosed in speech marks? Make sure there are no quote marks for thoughts. Have you got question marks, exclamation marks, commas and full stops in the correct space?

+ Have you used the correct tense? Don't change from past to present tense throughout the story or vice versa – unless you are doing it deliberately for a reason.

When you have done all this, check the following things:

+ Is the title appealing enough and does it reflect the content of the story?

+ Does the beginning grab the reader's attention and hold it?

+ Is your story the right length for your age group?

+ Is it presented correctly? We will deal with this next.

When you have checked all the above points, revised your work accordingly and are satisfied with it, then put it away for at least a week – longer if you can – so you can distance yourself from it. When you get it out again and read it you will see it with fresh eyes. It's amazing how many glaringly obvious mistakes you can miss because you are so familiar with the story.

Top tip

Don't revise your manuscript so much that you lose the original spark. It will never be perfect. When you've written it the best you can, then leave it alone!

HOW IMPORTANT IS GRAMMAR?

Whilst no one expects you to be an expert, your spelling and grammar do need to be of an acceptable standard. If they are really poor they will give a bad impression and make your work difficult to read so it will probably come winging back to you. If your grammar is a bit rusty buy yourself a grammar book. One written for children would teach you the basics in a simple way. If punctuation is your weak point then get a copy of Lynne Truss's amusing and effective *Eats, Shoots & Leaves*.

PRESENTING YOUR WORK

Editors are busy people and they receive hundreds of unsolicited manuscripts each week. Handwritten and badly presented work is not acceptable and will not be read. The guidelines for presenting your work are:

- Use a clear font like Times New Roman size 12, black ink and white A4 paper. An editor won't appreciate coloured paper, fancy fonts or small typefaces that make their eyes strain.

- Use double line spacing for your manuscript and type on one side of the page only, using left justification. Use single line spacing for your synopsis and cover letter.

- Leave wide margins at each side of the page. My margins are set to the normal Word format of 2.54 cm all around.

- Number your pages consecutively. Don't start on page one again for each chapter.

+ Write your name and your manuscript title at the top of each page.

+ Indent your paragraphs apart from the opening one of each chapter and use tabs to indent. I have my tab indent set to 1.27 cm.

+ Start a new page for each chapter and clearly number your chapters.

+ Include a cover sheet and a cover letter with your submission.

CREATING THE COVER SHEET

The job of the cover sheet is to let the editor know at a glance the title of your book, the age group, your name and contact details – and to keep your manuscript clean and tidy.

Here is a cover sheet template:

Book Title
By
Author

Catchy sentence describing genre and word length

Your name
Address
Phone number
Email

CREATING THE COVER LETTER

Keep your cover letter concise, to the point and business-like.

Don't tell the editor your life story, sing your own praises or tell them how much your children, friend's children and great aunt enjoyed reading your story or that you are taking a writing course. Don't ask them for advice on how to improve your story or on publishing in general. Editors are too busy to comment on all the manuscripts they receive. And definitely don't discuss copyright, royalties and payment at this stage. The time to do this is when you have sold your book.

Do tell the editor, briefly, what your book is about and the age range you are aiming at (no more than a couple of sentences), how long the finished book will be, your publishing record (if you have one) and why you have decided to send it to them. You could mention here that you notice from their website that they publish science-fiction stories (if you're sending a sci-fi text) and where you think your book will fit into their list. Do thank them for their time and say you appreciate any feedback they can give.

> **Top tip**
>
> Be concise. Keep your cover letter to one side of A4 paper.

AGENTS OR PUBLISHERS?

This is the 'chicken and egg' question as many publishers will no longer accept unagented work so they will be closed to you unless you have an agent. However, many agents prefer an author to have a track record before taking them on their books. It can actually be easier nowadays to get a publisher than get an agent, and many authors prefer to go it alone, believing it gives them more control over their work.

What does an agent do?

An agent's job is to sell your work for you, and to get you more work if they can. If they take you on they will read your work carefully and suggest places for revision, if needed. Then they will approach publishers on your behalf, send your manuscript to them, chase it up, vet your contract and haggle over your royalties and rights – often getting you a better deal than you can yourself. Obviously, an agent doesn't work for free so will charge you a commission of 10–15 per cent for this, and more for foreign sales. I think the main advantages to having an agent are:

1 Publishers know that work submitted by an agent is of a professional standard so they will read it and respond more quickly.

2 An agent is on your side. They will fight your corner with the publisher and deal with the money side of things, which many authors hate to do. If your advance or royalties are late, your agent will deal with it.

3 An agent can get you foreign sales and deal with the contracts and overseas rights for you.

4 Publishers will often approach an agent if they are looking for

writers for a project, so you get to have a go at it first. Agents can also obtain guidelines of what publishers are looking for and again can pass this information on to their writers.

The main disadvantages are that you have to pay an agent some of your hard-earned money and you lose the personal contact with the editor that you would have if you worked directly with them.

CHOOSING AN AGENT

The best way to choose an agent is to go on to agency websites and take a look at the agents' profiles, their clients, the sort of work they represent, their terms and their submission guidelines. Make sure that they represent children's authors, are looking for new clients and accept work in the genre in which you are writing. It's no use sending a picture-book manuscript to an agent that only deals with YA fiction. You can find a list of agents in the *Writers' and Artists' Yearbook* published by A & C Black. An internet search will also provide you with a list of agents' websites. If an agent appeals to you then follow the guidelines on their website about submitting work. Some agency websites state that they are closed to unsolicited submissions. If you really feel that one of the individual agents is the one with whom you would like to work, then you can sometimes sidestep the Submissions Department by writing specifically to your chosen agent. Tell them briefly what your book is about and why you think they are the best person to represent your work. The agent themselves may then choose to read your submission despite the general 'no submissions' policy.

CHOOSING A PUBLISHER

Do your research and check the publishers' websites to make sure that they publish children's books, and in the genre in which you are writing. Make sure that they aren't already publishing a very similar title to yours and that your title would fit into their list. Check their submission requirements to see if they are accepting unsolicited submissions and whether you should submit by post or email. Some publishers are only open to submissions at certain times of the year; if the website states that the publisher only accepts submissions between April and June then don't submit your manuscript in August. It will remain unread. The UK Children's Books website (www.ukchildrensbooks.co.uk/pubs.html) lists some children's publishers in the UK.

WHAT PUBLISHERS ARE LOOKING FOR

I put this question to the editorial department of Top That! Publishing and this was the response:

> Top That! receive hundreds of manuscripts each week so we look for text that stands out from the crowd, is a little different and keeps you reading from the first word. However, authors that send in their manuscripts need to have researched our company, the books we currently produce and to make a judgement as to if their manuscript would make a good fit. We also prefer a detailed synopsis as well as the first few chapters or full text.

SENDING OUT YOUR WORK

Check the agent's or publisher's website for guidelines on how to submit your work. If the agent or publisher wants postal submission then under no circumstances submit your work by email. It will just be deleted.

Sending postal submissions

+ Secure your manuscript with a paper clip or elastic band. Don't staple it together; apart from the fact that staples could prick the editor's finger they often photocopy a promising manuscript to pass to other people to read.

+ Fancy folders aren't appreciated and plastic folders can be slippery, especially when piled up on an editor's desk. If you must use a folder make it a cardboard wallet folder, clearly marked with the name of your manuscript, your own name and contact details.

+ Send a cover sheet and a cover letter with your manuscript. Enclose return postage.

Sending email submissions

Some agents/editors will accept email submissions. Again, study their guidelines for how to do this; check if they will accept attachments or prefer for the synopsis and sample chapters to be pasted into the email. Some publishers ask you to fill in a submission form and upload your files directly to their website. It's important that you adhere to their guidelines. Remember, though, that even when submitting by email you should stick to the normal presentation rules above unless the guidelines state otherwise.

WRITING THE QUERY LETTER

If a publisher states that they don't accept unagented submissions and you don't have an agent but really believe that your work is suitable for their list, then you could approach them with a query letter. In the letter mention the title of your book, briefly what it's about, the age group it's aimed at, your publishing credentials (if any), where you think it will fit into their list and ask them if they would consider it. Be polite, professional and business-like. If the publisher agrees to consider your work then you will have a contact name too. Never send unsolicited work to a publisher who doesn't accept it as your work won't be read.

> **Top tip**
>
> A query letter is a bit like a cover letter, but instead of enclosing your work you are asking the editor for permission to send it. So you need to make your book sound as interesting as you can, but be realistic – don't beef it up.

Sending email queries

Some publishers will accept queries by email. If this is the case, check the format and layout in which they want you to send your query. Write your email as professionally as you would a letter, addressing it correctly and checking it for errors.

Sending simultaneous and multiple submissions

At one time it was frowned upon to send your work out to different publishers at the same time, but nowadays editors can take many months to read your work so it's quite an acceptable practice. Check on the publisher's website first to see if they consider simultaneous submissions – if they don't then you have to decide whether to send your work solely to them and wait for their reply, or whether to cross them off your list.

Most publishers prefer you not to send them multiple submissions, i.e. sending them several works at the same time. I would advise you not to do this. Send your strongest work and if the publisher is interested in seeing anything else they will let you know.

AVOIDING THE SLUSH PILE

You might have heard of the term 'the slush pile'. This is basically the pile of unsolicited manuscripts that publishers receive – hundreds every week. The huge number of manuscripts means that many editors no longer have time to read them all so a reader is usually appointed to wade through them, shift out any that they think are promising and pass them on to the editor. This makes it even more essential that you only send your very best work and that it is neatly presented. This is your one and only chance to impress the reader and if you don't achieve that the editor won't even get to see the work. Don't waste it by sending first drafts, dog-eared manuscripts or messy, badly spelt or presented work.

PLAYING THE WAITING GAME

Most publishers' websites will have details of how long it takes them to reply to submissions. Some will state that they will only contact you if they are interested in your work so if you don't hear within a certain time (often two to three months), take it they aren't interested. Others will say it can take them up to six months to reply. This is why it's acceptable to send out simultaneous submissions. I wouldn't advise that you chase up a publisher until three months have passed, and then only make a general enquiry to check that they have received your submission and ask if they have any idea when they may have time to read it. Don't pressure them or you will simply get a rejection.

PUBLISHING GLOBALLY

Thanks to the internet, it's a small world and you're no longer restricted to only submitting work to UK publishers. Publishers Global (www.publishersglobal.com/directory/subject/children-publishers) lists some children's publishers globally, and the Verla Kay website (www.verlakay.com) gives lots of tips for children's writers including information about agents and publishers seeking submissions.

If you are thinking of working for an overseas publisher, especially one you haven't heard of before, then do check how long the publishing company has been going and that they are reputable (also see the 'Warning!' section on page 131).

Moira, a children's author who often works for overseas publishers, gives this advice:

I've had some great experiences with foreign publishers but also difficult times, especially when it comes to payment. Sometimes complicated tax forms must be filled in, and in the event of late payment you cannot go down a legal route easily if your contract is with a foreign-registered company. The best thing to do is to get your contract checked by the Society of Authors, if you are a member. Go into it with your eyes open, aware that if things go wrong you may not get easy redress. Check around to find out what others know about the company and check with your accountant what tax forms you need.

> **Top tip**
>
> It can be difficult to chase money owed from an overseas publisher. I've been informed that if your contract has a UK address you can get some redress through the courts over here, so this is a point worth checking.

Warning!

Be wary of agents who charge a fee for reading your work or publishers who ask you to pay towards publication of your work. A reputable agent reads your work for free and a reputable publisher pays you for publishing your work. Unfortunately, there are a few scams about, so check the small print before you sign up with an agent or publisher – apart from the big, well-known ones, of course. The Science Fiction and Fantasy Writers of America have a page on their website to alert writers about 'Schemes, Scams and Pitfalls' that threaten writers called – appropriately – Writer Beware (www. sfwa.org/for-authors/writer-beware).

SUMMING UP

- Never, ever send your first draft. Read through and revise your work several times.

- If you decide to get an agent, don't send the same work out to publishers as well.

- Do your research and make sure your work is suitable for the agent or publisher to whom you are sending it.

- Make sure your cover/query letter sounds business-like and is professionally presented.

- Don't email your work if the publisher only accepts postal submissions.

12

Rejections and Rewrites

REJECTING THE FAMOUS

Every writer I know has had their work rejected. It's part and parcel of a writer's life. Most people are familiar with the fact that J. K. Rowling's *Harry Potter and the Philosopher's Stone* was rejected by several publishers before Bloomsbury finally decided to publish it. Dr Seuss's *The Cat in the Hat* was also rejected many times, with one publisher saying that it was 'too different from other juveniles on the market to warrant its selling'. *The Wind in the Willows* by Kenneth Grahame was turned down because it was considered 'an irresponsible holiday story', and *Watership Down* by Richard Adams was turned down because the publisher thought that its language was too difficult.

These examples were taken from Andrew Bernard's book, *Rotten Rejections*. You can also find them on the Writers Services website (www.writersservices.com/mag/m_rejection.htm).

DEALING WITH REJECTIONS

The important thing to remember is that there will always be someone who doesn't like your work. So don't be disheartened if you receive a rejection letter. Don't put your manuscript away in a fit of pique and vow never to write again. Instead, go and make yourself a cup of tea or coffee (or something stronger!), nibble on a chocolate biscuit and read through some of the rejections on the website above to cheer yourself up. Then take a look at the letter again.

Is it a standard rejection letter?

If it is, then ask yourself the following questions:

1　Has the editor written anything like 'this does not fit into our list' or 'we suggest that you study our website to see the kind of books we publish'? If so, you haven't done your research thoroughly enough and have sent your book to the wrong publisher. Always check the guidelines and study the range of books on the publisher's website before sending your work to them.

2　Are you sure that your book is the very best it can be? Read it over again. Is it presented correctly and error free? Editors will always reject sloppy work, often without reading it.

3　Is it too similar to a book they already publish or to a well-known book? The successes of *Harry Potter* and the *Twilight* series have both inspired lots of authors to write in a similar vein. The market can get too saturated with a certain type of book, so it will be turned down no matter if it is well written.

4　Is your book too moralistic or old-fashioned? Many new authors write the sort of book they liked reading as a child, in exactly the same tone. This dates their work and makes it boring to children today. Similarly, if your tone is too preachy it can be off-putting. Remember, children want to be entertained, not preached at.

If none of the above applies to you then it could be simply that your book isn't what the publisher is looking for. Assessing the quality of a book can be subjective; it often depends on the opinion of the person reading it. So research another publisher, type out a fresh letter, put your manuscript in another envelope and send it off.

If the editor has made some comments about your book

Rejoice! The editor has seen some promise in your work, enough to make them take time out from their very busy schedule to give you some personal feedback. You may not like the feedback. The editor could be suggesting you omit a passage you love, tweak the ending, make the story shorter. Whatever the suggestion, let go of your pride and listen. Consider the editor's remarks carefully. Ask yourself if they could be right. If you still disagree then send out your work to another publisher. If it comes back again with similar comments I suggest you take heed. A comment made once is an editor's opinion and can be ignored if you wish; the same comment repeated reveals, I think, a weakness in your work. I would suggest that you take the comment on board and revise your work accordingly.

However, it's your story, so if you still don't agree with the comments then continue sending your work out. As I mentioned earlier, many well-known books were rejected. It could be that you haven't found the right home for your book yet. Persevere.

KEEPING RECORDS

It's a good idea to keep a record of the publishers to whom you send your book – that way you can ensure that you don't send it to the same publisher twice. Either a notebook or spreadsheet will do. Write the name of the publisher, the name of the editor to whom you sent it (if you were given one; many publishers tell you to address your submission to the submissions department), the date you sent it, the date you received a reply and what the reply was. That way you can keep check on how long your manuscript has been out, the number of times you have sent it out and any comments you have received.

WRITING REVISIONS

Sometimes an editor will see potential in your work and write to you suggesting that you make some revisions to it. They may or may not ask to see it again once you have made these revisions. There are two common reactions to this: wounded pride that they don't like your precious work exactly how you've written it or joy that the editor likes your work and will publish it if you do the revisions. Be careful with both reactions. Your pride could prevent you from seeing that what the editor is suggesting is right. However, your assumption that the editor will publish your work as soon as you have revised it could be wrong. The editor might just be giving you advice because they think your work shows promise.

Has the editor asked to see the revised work?

Take a look at the letter again. Does the editor actually ask to see your work again once you have made the revisions? If so, then they have definitely seen some potential in your manuscript. But don't take it as a guarantee that it will be published. The editor is suggesting revisions and a second read, not offering publication. So don't get excited just yet. Do give yourself a pat on the back, though, that your work shows enough promise to prompt a busy editor giving so much of their time to suggest ways of improving it.

If the editor hasn't requested to see the revised work

The editor has suggested revisions but hasn't asked to see your book again. What do you do? I would suggest that you send a polite letter thanking the editor for the suggestions. State that you are revising your work according to the comments and wonder if they would be willing to read it again when you have finished. If the editor says yes, great. Post it off and keep your fingers crossed. If they don't reply or say no, do the revisions anyway and send it somewhere else. And don't let this stop you from sending the editor any future work. It could be that this book isn't suitable for the publishing list but because your work showed potential they decided to give you some advice. Your next book might be just the thing for which the editor is looking.

WHAT IF IT'S STILL REJECTED?

Editors might reject your book even if you have revised it exactly how you were asked. They might decide that it still doesn't work. Or they might suggest further revisions and then finally reject the book. It's frustrating but it happens. Publishers are in the business to make money; they generally know what sells and they will know what they are looking for. Sadly, even after many tweaks your book might not be it. All you can do is take heart that you now have (hopefully) a more polished manuscript, thank the editor politely for their time and send it off somewhere else.

WHEN TO GIVE UP

You've sent your book to every children's publisher in the *Writers' and Artists' Yearbook* and still not found it a home. What do you do?

If you have had some kind comments about your book I would suggest putting it away for a little while. The time might not be right for it. Markets and moods change and in a few years' time your book might come into its own.

If you have only received standard rejection letters, and sometimes no reply at all, then I would put your book in the bottom drawer, forget all about it and start writing the next one. Most authors have a few manuscripts gathering dust that will probably never get published. It's all part of the learning curve. To be a writer you have to write, and sometimes your earlier work is writing practice. Don't regard it as having wasted your time. Practice makes perfect and sometimes you need to write a book or two so that you can learn to hone your skills enough to write a book that will be published. Whatever you do, don't throw it away or shred it. In a few years' time you might read it again and see a way that you can rewrite it or at least use the idea to write something else.

GETTING ON WITH THE NEXT BOOK

Editors and agents want writers who have a career in front of them, not one-book wonders. As soon as you have finished one book and sent it off, start on another. It will keep your mind from constantly wondering how your book is faring and biting your fingernails down to the core whilst you wait for a decision. Further, if your first book does get rejected then you will have another one ready to send out, which will stop you feeling so disheartened.

If you truly want to be a writer then never give up. As Richard Bach said, 'A professional writer is an amateur who didn't quit.'

SUMMING UP

+ If your work is rejected, check it over. Can you see anything glaringly wrong with it?

+ Read the editor's letter carefully. Do they suggest any rewrites? Do you agree with them?

+ If you are happy with your work, send it out again.

+ Keep a record of the names of publishers to whom you have sent your work.

+ Don't give up. Ever.

13

Published – What Next?

BEING ACCEPTED AT LAST!

The day you have dreamed about has finally arrived. You've had an offer for your book. You're finally going to be a published author. Your first instinct will probably be to leap up in the air, hug any family member or friend who's around, phone up those who aren't and go on to Facebook or Twitter to tell the rest of the world. You will, for a while, feel on top of the world.

Then you'll calm down and read the letter again. You might find that the editor wants you to do some revisions and that your contract is on the condition that you comply with these. This might upset you if you like your story just the way it is and don't want to make any alterations to it. As I said in the previous chapter, I suggest that you think carefully about this. The editor knows the market; they will want your book to be a success and believe that the changes they are suggesting will make it sell better.

If there are some changes you could go along with but a couple you feel really strongly about, then my advice would be to see if you can come to a compromise. Contact the editor and tell them your concerns, explaining that while you are quite happy to go along with most of their suggestions there are a couple of things you don't want to alter. Give them strong reasons why. Be professional and calm. Most editors want to keep their authors happy and will listen to you, but they also want to make money from your book and if they think the changes are for the best they will insist upon them. So it's up to you whether you give way because you want your book to be published or stick to your ethics and take your book elsewhere. It's your story at the end of the day so the final decision is yours.

GETTING PAID

There are two sorts of contract, fixed fee or royalties.

The fixed fee contract. This means that you receive a one-off fee for your book. You can still get PLR (Public Lending Rights) payments if you are named as the author but you won't receive royalties. Fixed fee contracts are the standard for licensed character works and they are used by many packagers.

The royalty contract. This is the contract most authors prefer. It means you get an advance against royalties and then a percentage of every book that sells. This is usually 5–10 per cent but can be significantly lower if your books are sold cheaper through book clubs or discount stores. Royalty payments are made every six months, usually in March and September, but the dates can vary depending on the publisher.

I, and many authors I know, work on both fixed fee and royalty contract terms depending on the circumstances.

SIGNING THE CONTRACT

A contract can vary between a single page (usually for fixed fee work) and over a dozen very complicated pages. Fixed fee contracts are fairly simple but royalty contracts are more difficult to understand. If you have got an agent they will negotiate the contract for you, agreeing an advance, the amount of free (gratis) copies you get, the percentage of royalty, subsidiary and overseas rights, etc. If you haven't got an agent then I suggest that you join the Society of Authors (www.societyofauthors.net). Membership is open to anyone who has a book published or a contract for a book (providing they haven't contributed to the cost), and you can ask them to read it for you.

The contract might also state that the publisher wants the first option on your next book, which means that you offer it to them first. If they don't want it you're free to offer it elsewhere. This is simply because a publisher invests a lot of money in an author and doesn't want a one-hit wonder; they're hoping that you'll have a long career with them. It doesn't always work out that way, of course, as no one can predict how well a book will sell or how popular an author will be.

The contract may also ask you to agree not to write a similar book for anyone else. This doesn't mean that you can't work for another publisher, just that you can't write a competing title. If you sell a fantasy story to one publisher you can write a historical one for another.

RECEIVING FREE COPIES

Your contract will state how many 'gratis' copies of your book you'll receive, usually between six and ten. There will also be a clause in your contract allowing you to purchase your books at a discounted price, usually 25–50 per cent. This is for personal use only, for you to give to family and friends or send out as a sample of your work. Many publishers often extend this discount to any of the books they publish, which can be a very useful saving.

> **Top tip**
>
> Read your contract carefully. Never sign anything you don't understand. Always ask for advice.

USING A PEN NAME

Your contract will probably ask if you're using a pseudonym or pen name. Some authors do, some don't. You might want to use one for several reasons:

+ You don't like your own name, it's difficult to pronounce or is very long.

+ You don't think your name will appeal to your audience. For example, J. K. Rowling used her initials instead of her Christian name so that she would sound like a man and thus appeal to boys too.

+ You'd like a name to suit the title and theme of your book. American Writer Daniel Handler chose the name Lemony

Snicket for his *Unfortunate Events* series. I'm sure you'll agree that Lemony Snicket is far more memorable!

+ Your name is too similar to a well-known author. If your name is Jacqueline Wilson you would probably be asked to change it, even if it was only to Jackie Wilson.

+ You are already published under one name and want to choose another one because you're writing for a different market, genre or publisher. I write children's books under my own name of Karen King but romantic fiction under the name of Kay Harborne (K is my initial and Harborne is my mother's maiden name).

The contract will be in your real name and will state that you're writing under a pseudonym, with details of this.

After signing your contract a long time will pass. You might even think that your editor has forgotten all about your book but lots of things will be happening at the publishers. Finally, things will pass on to the next stages, involving the illustrations, book cover and proofs – not necessarily in that order.

ARRANGING ILLUSTRATIONS

If your book requires illustrations then your editor will arrange this. Publishers have a list of artists whom they use and will match up with your work. They will hope that you like the artwork but, in my experience, if you don't it's tough. The editor's decision is final – unless, of course, you're a well-known author with a lot of clout.

There are some author and artist teams that work together but it's probable that you will never get to meet the artist connected to your book. The only occasion I ever met an artist with whom I was working was when we were both in London on the same day – seeing different publishers – and decided to meet up for lunch. So be prepared for artwork samples to be posted or emailed to you. You will be asked to check for any glaring mistakes such as your character having wavy, blonde hair and the girl in the pictures having straight black hair (it happens, honest!). Apart from that ,you probably won't have much input.

DESIGNING THE BOOK COVER

It's the same with book covers. You might be asked to provide a blurb or it could be done in-house by the editor. You're not likely to be asked what you would like on the cover; rather, the design will be sent to you – probably by email. If you don't like it, it's highly unlikely you can reject it, but do tell the editor if you really have strong reasons: perhaps the character or setting looks nothing like the one in your story, or the cover makes the book look like a romance and it's actually a supernatural thriller. A sympathetic editor might allow some changes, but don't be surprised if they ask you to alter your character or setting to fit the cover. Artwork is expensive and editors are always looking to save costs.

EDITING PROOFS

Finally, you'll receive the proofs of your book. These are usually sent by email now, and you'll be expected to write any amendments directly on to the file. This isn't the time to make drastic alterations to your plot; in fact, your contract will probably only allow you to make a certain amount of alterations before you are charged for them. So look out for inconsistencies, typos and grammar mistakes. Read your work slowly to make sure that you spot the errors – if you skim-read, your eyes will only see what they expect to see. I usually select the show/hide button on the Word menu bar so that all the spaces show up, as it makes me read more carefully. Other authors use a piece of paper or ruler to cover all the other lines as they work their way down the page. You will be given a deadline for reading and returning the proofs – usually about ten to twenty-one days.

PUBLICIZING AND MARKETING

Your publisher has a publicity department to handle the publicity and marketing of your book. They may send advance proof copies to reviewers, newspapers, magazines and websites that specialize in children's books. They may also contact your local newspaper and radio, or suggest that you do. Some authors aren't comfortable with giving interviews or publicizing their work but nowadays publishers expect you to do some self-promotion. You might find it easier to promote yourself using Twitter or Facebook – we'll talk more about this a little further on.

CREATING YOUR AUTHOR PLATFORM

An author platform is how you reach out and engage with your audience. It's not just about self-promotion and persuading people to buy your book; it's about having an online presence, contributing and commenting on blogs, being friendly, approachable and contactable. Interaction, apparently, is the keyword for building your author platform. There are a few tried and tested ways to do this:

Creating your website

Most authors nowadays have a website. They vary from a basic website that gives a bit of information about you and your work to a professional all-singing, all-dancing website with videos, interviews, clips of the author reading out from their book, book reviews and tips for writers. One way to encourage interaction with the book-buying audience is to put some writer's tips on your website, or a blog, or run a question-and-answer session. You don't have to pay a lot of money for a website; there are some free ones you can use, such as MoonFruit (www.moonfruit.com) and Weebly (www.weebly.com) if you don't mind a few adverts on your pages. You can drop the adverts by paying for an upgraded version.

Using Twitter

For those new to using Twitter it is basically a form of communication with people in messages under 140 characters long. It's used by celebrities as a method of tweeting news of their latest releases, high jinks or thoughts to their fans, and by people all the world over to communicate.

At the time of writing this book, Twitter is still popular for keeping in contact with readers and fans, promoting your book and letting people know what you're working on now. Many writers use it to advertise interviews or book signings they're doing or to link to good reviews that they have received.

If you are an avid Twitter user yourself and are considering using it for promotion, be careful. Nicola Morgan, author of the ebook *Tweet Right*, advises against using Twitter solely for self-promotion and marketing. She believes that too much self-promotion and marketing is off-putting, saying, 'People don't like being marketed at on Twitter, any more than they'd like it if you bounced up to them in a bar and started going on about your latest idea. In fact, many people I know will block companies who follow them. And they will "unfollow" or even block people who keep banging on about how fantastic they are.'

I am on Twitter (you can find me at @karen_king) but I confess that I'm not a big fan of it and rarely tweet. I find it too time-consuming. I know that a lot of authors find it invaluable, though. Some authors even tweet sections of their book or tell the whole story in tweets. If you want to know more about using Twitter effectively then I suggest that you buy *Tweet Right*. It's full of useful information and is written in an approachable, no-nonsense style.

If you haven't got a Twitter account simply go to https://twitter.com to sign up.

Using Facebook

Most people now use Facebook as a way of communicating with their families and friends. I wouldn't advise using your normal Facebook page for communicating with your fans – it's not a good idea to share details about your personal life with them. However, many authors have a Facebook author page where they keep their fans up to date with things of interest such as events, workshops, interviews, the new book they're working on, etc. People can also comment and contact them on this page, which encourages interaction with the author.

To create a Facebook author page simply log in to your Facebook account and go to this link: https://www.facebook.com/#!/pages/create.php. If it doesn't work (Facebook is constantly changing!), go to the help section and type in 'create a page'. You'll be given a choice of pages: click on the artist one, then select author or writer, click the box to accept the Facebook terms and conditions then follow the on-screen instructions to create your page. I recommend that you upload a picture as it looks friendlier; if you don't want to use a photograph of yourself then use a book cover or a logo. Now ask your friends to 'like' your new professional page. As this will be a public page I don't advise putting too much information on it – only put what you're happy for everyone to see. You can go to my Facebook author page at https://www.facebook.com/#!/KarenKingAuthor if you want to see a sample page.

> ### Top tip
>
> Put your author Facebook page and website address in the signature line of your email. Then it will automatically appear on every email you write.

RECEIVING ADVANCE COPIES

Receiving your advance copies will be a very exciting time for you. They will probably arrive a couple of weeks before publication day. Sometimes, though, there can be a delay in receiving your advance copies. I was talking to some children in assembly at a school I was visiting when the headmistress told me some supplies of my books had arrived that morning. She handed me them to sign in front of the whole school. Imagine my surprise when I noticed my latest picture book among them – I hadn't even received my advance copy of it! 'Gosh, I haven't seen that myself yet!' I said. The headmistress was thrilled and insisted on taking a photo of me looking at my newly published book for the very first time.

PUBLICATION DAY!

The day you've been waiting for has finally arrived. Your book is being published. This is a very important day for you but it isn't anything special for your publisher – unless your book is the 'next big thing' and you've been given a huge advance and shedloads of publicity. Hundreds of books are published in the UK every week; yours is just one of them so don't expect to be front – or even back – page news. Some publishers might throw a launch party for you, others might send you a card and some publishers will do nothing at all.

BOOK SIGNINGS

Your publicist might arrange for you to do some book signings at local bookstores, or you could arrange them yourself if you want to publicize your new book. I don't know of any authors who enjoy these. Unless you're a household name you're not likely to attract a crowd queuing around the block and could find yourself sitting like 'Billy No Mates' at a table full of unsold books. If you find yourself roped into doing a book signing I would suggest doing the following things:

+ Take along some free sweets, pencils or bookmarks to attract children to your table.

+ Bribe, beg and coerce your family and friends to come along and give you support.

+ Take a book to read or a pad to write on to keep yourself occupied.

+ Keep smiling! If you look friendly and approachable you might attract a bit of attention.

BEING INTERVIEWED

Your publicist might also arrange for you to be interviewed by your local newspaper or radio. Be prepared – think about what you're going to say. It's a good idea to prepare a press release for the paper so the reporter has the facts written down, then all they have to do is take your photo. For the radio, try to think of the sort of questions they will ask. Here are some typical ones, not necessarily in this order:

+ When did you start writing?

+ Why did you want to be a writer?

+ Did you have many rejections?

+ What is your book about?

+ What inspired you to write it?

+ Who is your favourite author?

+ What's your next book about?

If you're prepared you'll feel more relaxed. Remember to take a deep breath before you go on air, listen carefully to the questions and answer slowly and clearly.

PROMOTING YOUR BOOK IN OTHER WAYS

There are a few other ways you can promote your book without too much expenditure.

Creating bookmarks or leaflets

You could create these yourself on your computer, using a programme like Publisher. Include your book cover, a brief blurb about your book, your website URL and email address. You could sign the bookmarks if you want them to be more personal. You'll probably get four bookmarks per A4 page. Print them out on thin card and cut into separate bookmarks. Alternatively, you could use paper and laminate them for a more professional finish.

Similarly, you could design some leaflets with a picture, brief blurb and perhaps an extract from your book. Don't forget to give your contact details.

Alternatively, if you want a more professional finish, you could order bookmarks, leaflets and business cards from an online printer such as Vistaprint, who have templates to make designing them easier for you. You can also get promotional pens and pencils quite cheaply.

Arranging storytelling sessions

You could contact your local library or bookshop and offer to give a free storytelling session to promote your book. If you have written a picture book, or one just a couple of thousand words long, you could read that in a half-hour session. If it's a longer book then just read the first couple of chapters to whet your audience's appetite. Take a few books with you in case anyone wants to buy one, and a few bookmarks, if you have any, for the children to take away with them.

Conducting school visits

Some authors like visiting schools, some don't. Personally, I love it and often work with a school for a whole day, talking to the children about my writing and running workshops. You might not fancy this and it certainly isn't compulsory. If you'd like to do it and don't know how to get started, try contacting your local school to see if they would like you to visit them to talk about your work. Schools usually love visits from authors, and you could keep the visit short, perhaps just half an hour, until you feel more comfortable doing it. It will give you the chance to talk about your book and maybe even sell a few copies. If it goes well you could contact another local school to see if they would like you to visit them. Once you get a bit or experience under your belt you could contact schools further afield and do half- or full-day visits.

SUMMING UP

- Read your contract carefully and get advice if you don't understand it.

- Decide if you want to be published under a pen name or your real name.

- Don't make major changes at the proofs stage.

- Be prepared to help promote your book.

- Enjoy it! This is the moment you've been waiting for.

14

E-publishing and Self-publishing

Thanks to the growing sales of iPads, Kindles, Kobos and other electronic reading devices, e-publishing has become increasingly popular, even overtaking print publishing in some areas. If you sell a book to a traditional publisher the chances are that they will also publish an electronic version.

The advantages of e-publishing are that it's quicker, cheaper and more accessible. Readers can download your book on to any number of devices including their computer, smartphone or tablet if they haven't got an e-reader. Royalties are higher for ebooks and the audience is global. Anyone can download your book instantly from anywhere in the world.

The disadvantages are that an ebook is technically a file not a book. You can't line your bookshelves with ebooks, hold book-signing sessions or sell them on school visits. However, I believe there's a place for both ebooks and printed books, and I am happy to be published either way. My YA book *Perfect Summer* was initially published just as an ebook by the American e-publisher Astraea Press. I have to admit, though, that whilst I love the versatility and huge memory of an e-reader, which allows me to take a whole library of books on holiday, nothing beats the feel of a book in my hand.

You can either publish through an e-publisher, or publish it yourself on an e-platform such as Kindle or Smashwords. Let's take a look at e-publishers first.

WHAT DO E-PUBLISHERS DO?

E-publishers do pretty much the same as a traditional publisher but your work is published as an electronic file instead of a printed book. An e-publisher has a website, a bookstore where they sell the books, a publicist, editors, designers – the whole works. You'll get a contract telling you what rights they want and for how long. You probably won't get an advance but royalties are much higher than printed books because of the low overheads.

How do you submit your work?

The publisher's website should have details. A synopsis and the first three chapters is still standard for a longer book. Some ask for submissions with double line spacing, some with 1.5 and some with single line spacing. Read the guidelines carefully. If your book is accepted for publication you will probably be sent further 'house' guidelines for formatting your work.

E-publishers are just as professional as print publishers

Some people mistakenly look on e-publishing as an easier option. Anyone who has worked for an e-publisher will tell you that this is not true. Professional e-publishers take as much pride in their work as traditional ones. You will be assigned an editor with whom to work, and sent proofs and cover designs just as with a print publisher.

Do the books ever go into print?

Yes. Some e-publishers have a clause in their contract that when a certain number of books have been sold they will do a print run. If the e-publisher doesn't deal with printed books and your book is popular, then a traditional publisher might pick it up. But don't take it for granted that your book will eventually be printed; if you have a contract for an ebook then that is all you should expect.

SELF-PUBLISHING

Some authors prefer to go down the self-publishing route for various reasons. The main drawback to this is that you're responsible for your own editing, marketing and publicity. The main advantage, of course, is that any money you make is your own once you have cleared your overheads.

DOING YOUR OWN E-PUBLISHING

Self-publishing ebooks is very popular with new authors and gaining popularity with professional ones. I've spoken to some traditionally published authors and found that the main reasons that they have turned to self-publishing an ebook are either because their book didn't fit into the standard publishing format – the children's market can be particularly restricting – or their published books are now out of print and they want to reach a whole new audience. I e-published my children's fantasy novel, *Firstborn*, on Amazon Kindle as an experiment to see how it would do, and also e-published a romance novel, *Never Say*

Forever, which is still available as a printed book. Make sure that you own the digital rights if you intend to e-publish a book that is still in print.

Before starting

You should approach writing and publishing your own ebook just as professionally as you would if you were sending your work to a publisher. Make sure that your story is the very best you can write it and that there are no grammar, spelling or punctuation errors. I would recommend that you pay for the services of an editor to go through it for you. If money is tight then make sure that you check it over very thoroughly several times, putting it away for a while between each read through to ensure you read it with fresh eyes. Perhaps you could ask a couple of writer friends to check it over too, although this is no match for a professional edit. Be thorough: don't rush this essential part of the procedure. Errors can be easily spotted on a small screen such as a mobile phone or an e-reader and your readers will be disappointed if your work is slipshod.

Setting out your manuscript

The format for ebooks is slightly different than for printed books. The important thing to remember is that e-readers come in different sizes so it's best to keep the layout and format simple to ensure it works on a variety of screens and devices. Here are some general rules:

+ Don't number your pages as the pages will adjust according to the screen size of the e-reader and the settings that the readers themselves choose.

+ Don't use headers or footers as they look odd on a small screen.

+ Do use standard fonts such as Times New Roman or Ariel, with left alignment.

+ Use single line spacing as double line spacing means a lot of space between text on a small screen.

+ Make sure there are no blank spaces or blank pages as they really show up on an e-screen.

+ Check that you've only left one space between words and at the end of sentences. I always click on the 'show' icon on the Word toolbar as this marks the space between words with a dot thus making it easy for me to see if I have an extra space.

+ Indent the beginning of each new paragraph so the reader can see where it begins.

+ Use the 'page break' option on your Word toolbar or press 'ctrl' and 'enter' simultaneously to insert page breaks rather than hitting the enter key until you get to the end of the page.

+ Avoid using tabs and keep formatting to a minimum.

I'm not an expert on e-publishing so for more detailed information buy a book to guide you, such as *Make an eBook* by Michael Boxwell. It's important that you get it right.

Other things you need to do

There are a few other things that you are responsible for doing when you self-publish an ebook:

The cover. The cover of your ebook is vitally important, so unless you're a talented artist don't attempt to do it yourself. And remember that the image will also need to look good in black and white and as a thumbnail size. I'm lucky enough to be able to use the services of my illustrator daughter, Namie King (www.nemki.co.uk). If you can't afford to pay an illustrator then Michael Boxwell suggests in *Make an eBook* that you visit the website http://fiverr. com where you may be able to find artists, and even professional designers, willing to design your book cover for £5. Michael states that he tried it out himself and was pleasantly surprised by the covers he was sent, so you might like to give it a try.

The copyright page. This is information that your publisher usually provides but now it's up to you. Don't panic, you just have to basically say something about the book being copyrighted by you and that no copying is permitted. Add a disclaimer that the characters and events are fictional. This is what I put at the beginning of *Firstborn:*

This is a work of fiction. The characters, dialogue and incidents are products of the author's imagination and are not to be considered as real. Any resemblance to any events or persons, living or dead, is purely coincidental.

With grateful thanks to Andres Alzate for designing the cover.

Feel free to reword this for your own use.

Author information. It's a good idea to end your ebook with a bit of information about yourself and a link to your website. You could also add a sample page of your next book with a link for the reader to click to download. Don't waffle, though; keep it short.

PUBLISHING ON KINDLE

Both my ebooks are published on Amazon Kindle. It's free and quite simple to use. Once your book is uploaded it's for sale on the Amazon website, both in the UK and overseas. You can also create a printed version by using their Create Space. Go to https://kindle.amazon.com for more details. You'll be given guides to formatting the book too.

USING SMASHWORDS

This is another free platform for e-publishing. I haven't used it myself but believe it works similar to Amazon. Smashwords distribute their books to places such as Barnes and Noble so they could possibly reach a wider audience. You can self-publish the same book on both Amazon and Smashwords providing you don't opt in to Amazon's KDP programme (a sort of online lending library). If you go to the website at www.smashwords.com you'll find advice on how to use the service.

PRINTING ON DEMAND/SELF-PUBLISHING PRINTED BOOKS

This is becoming increasingly popular amongst authors who want to publish their own works. In a nutshell, it means that the publisher only prints books when you have an order so one or two at a time can be printed. There are do-it-yourself internet-based companies such as Lulu (www.lulu.com) and Amazon's Create Space, which are relatively low-cost compared to more expensive publishing services. A traditional self-publisher will charge you a fee for printing a certain amount of copies of your books, usually a minimum of 200.

PAYING VANITY PUBLISHERS

Never pay a publisher to publish your book. Vanity publishers often promise the earth and charge you huge amounts to publish several hundred copies of your book, which will then be left cluttering up your garage. If you're thinking of going down this route, check out Writer Beware (www.sfwa.org/for-authors/writer-beware/vanity).

SELF-PUBLISHING MARKETING AND PUBLICITY

As I said earlier, if you self-publish – whether as an ebook, print-on-demand or traditional printed book – you are responsible for your own marketing and publicity. This can be a very time-consuming and expensive business so be prepared to put in long hours and for it to take some time to cover your costs.

SUMMING UP

+ When submitting your work to an e-publisher take as much care as you would for a traditional print publisher.

+ If you're self-publishing check your manuscript very carefully for any errors.

+ Employ an editor if you can afford it.

+ Don't create your own book cover unless you are a talented artist.

+ Be prepared to spend a lot of time and effort marketing your book.

Appendices

USEFUL INFORMATION

Arranging copyright

Everything you write is automatically your copyright as soon as you write it, so you don't have to do anything to register your copyright. There's no need to use the copyright symbol on your manuscript or post a copy of your book to yourself (or to a solicitor, as some writers do) and leave it unopened in the safe. Copyright remains with the writer for seventy years after their death. For more information about copyright, fair usage rights and quoting from other authors' work, check out the UK Copyright website at www.copyrightservice.co.uk/copyright/p01_uk_copyright_law.

Receiving Public Lending Rights payments

As soon as your book is published and has an ISBN you can register it on the Public Lending Rights (PLR) website (www.plr.uk.com), which gives you a legal right to payment when your book is taken out from libraries. You can register for both Irish and UK PLR on this website, but do it before the cut-off date of June every year if you want payments for that year. You have to be named as the author of the book but don't have to own the copyright. If your book has illustrations then you'll have to agree a share of PLR with the artists. The website will give you more details. Loans are based on data from a sample of libraries and are currently 6.20 pence per loan, so can be a useful boost to your income. PLR is usually paid out in February.

Receiving copy payments

This can be another useful top-up to your income. The Authors' Licensing and Collecting Society (ALCS) collects money for writers from practices such as photocopying, scanning and digital copying. This is especially useful if your books are used in schools. For more information look at its website (www.alcs.co.uk).

Entering prizes

There are several prizes awarded to the authors of children's books each year, the most popular being the Carnegie Medal and the Costa Book Award. You can find a list of prizes and awards on the Children's Literature Web Guide (http://people.ucalgary.ca/~dkbrown/awards.html).

Seeking funding

The four UK Arts Councils give grants to artists and writers to help them develop projects or to give them time to write. There are criteria to be met and a big demand for funding. Check out their websites for guidelines and also details of other funding available at www.artscouncil.org.uk; www.scottisharts.org.uk; www.artswales.org.uk; and www.artscouncil-ni.org.

Attending writing courses

There has been a boom in writing courses both at university level and through distance-learning courses over the past decade or so. Many people say that writers are born not taught, and I agree with this to a certain extent, but writers can be taught how to improve their work. I am a writing tutor and believe that my purpose is to pass on skills and tips I've learnt during my writing career so that my students can avoid making the mistakes I made and hopefully achieve a standard of work that could take them a few years to reach unaided. Having taught at university level, adult education courses and via distance learning I've seen the benefit that students have gained from the courses, with several going on to have books published. The structure and deadlines of a course can also motivate you as a writer.

Diana Nadin, Director of The Writers Bureau courses, says:

> I know some people still query whether writing can be taught, but if you enrol on a good course it will definitely give your career a push in the right direction. It will explain how the industry works; the best way to approach editors and publishers; how to get paid and how to avoid scams. In addition, the advice from your personal tutor (provided that tutor is an experienced writer) is invaluable. It will help you to improve your work, show you how to target your writing and ultimately save you time and heartache.

Do make sure that your course is an accredited one and read the details about the course carefully to make sure it's the right one for you.

Here's a list of some distance-learning courses:

The Arvon Foundation (www.arvonfoundation.org): Runs creative writing courses, including writing for children. Some grants are available.

The Writers Bureau (www.writersbureau.com): Distance-learning writing courses including one called 'Writing for Children', which covers all aspects of children's fiction, including picture books.

Open College of Arts (www.oca-uk.com): Runs various distance-learning courses including on writing for children.

London School of Journalism (www.lsj.org/web/dl.php): Offers a variety of courses, including a short course on writing for children.

International Correspondence School (www.icslearn.co.uk): Runs a short course called 'Writing Books for Children'.

If you want to study at university level then contact your local university to see if they offer a professional or creative writing course.

Words of wisdom

Looking for some words of wisdom to keep you motivated? Well, here is some advice from published authors:

> Write the first draft subjectively, with your heart, and the second objectively, with your head. Understand why publishers and agents make the decisions they do. Be informed, adaptable, opportunistic and brave. (Nicola Morgan)

Be prepared to work hard and still get rejections, to have ups and downs, to feel like nothing you write is working, because that is part of the landscape. The other side is when you discover that your characters and their story are loved by your readers, that it makes them want to read on when they are supposed to be doing something else or, better still, that it is the book that reached that one child when nothing else made them want to read. That is what makes it so wonderful – the best job in the world. (Linda Strachan)

Having ideas is easy. Wrestling them into a story that actually works is the hard part. And while you're wrestling, you can't be ill or exhausted or worried about something else. Writing requires what I call a 'selfish brain', which means there isn't room for anything other than STORY. This, to me, explains why it's possible to get a lot of writing done in a couple of hours, or alternatively none at all in a week of 'spare time'! (Jo Cotterill)

My advice to anyone wanting to write for children is to know what age group you are writing for and make sure the content of the story will grab their attention – and keep it. Then write and rewrite. As with any form of writing, you have to persevere. In my opinion writing for children is the best thing. There's nothing more rewarding than reading one of your own stories to a class of children and seeing their faces and their reaction. (Ann Evans)

Listen to the advice of experts: Accept criticism and act on same unless you profoundly disagree: See rejection slips as a challenge and act on any advice contained in same. Finally, have faith in your product. (Alan Cliff)

And finally, some words of wisdom from famous authors:

> Imagination is more important than knowledge. (Albert Einstein)

> If you don't have time to read, you don't have the time (or the tools) to write. Simple as that. (Stephen King)

> Substitute 'damn' every time you're inclined to write 'very'; your editor will delete it and the writing will be just as it should be. (Mark Twain)

> After nourishment, shelter and companionship, stories are the thing we need most in the world. (Philip Pullman)

> Tomorrow may be hell, but today was a good writing day, and on the good writing days nothing else matters. (Neil Gaiman)

> The first draft of anything is shit. (Ernest Hemingway)

> Write the kind of story you would like to read. People will give you all sorts of advice about writing, but if you are not writing something you like, no one else will like it either. (Meg Cabot)

> One always has a better book in one's mind than one can manage to get onto paper. (Michael Cunningham)

> Cut out all these exclamation points. An exclamation point is like laughing at your own joke. (F. Scott Fitzgerald)

> The reason that fiction is more interesting than any other form of literature, to those who really like to study people, is that in fiction the author can really tell the truth without humiliating himself. (Eleanor Roosevelt)

If you can tell stories, create characters, devise incidents, and have sincerity and passion, it doesn't matter a damn how you write. (W. Somerset Maugham)

Get it down. Take chances. It may be bad, but it's the only way you can do anything really good. (William Faulkner)

There's no such thing as writer's block. That was invented by people in California who couldn't write. (Terry Pratchett)

FAQs

Here are ten questions I'm often asked:

I have so many ideas I don't know which one to write first. How do I decide?

I often have this problem too, so I go for the idea that is shouting the loudest in my head – the one that keeps coming back and demanding to be written.

How many words should I write every day?

There's no rule for this (unless you're on a deadline!); write as many as you feel comfortable with. The important thing is to write every day, even if it's only a sentence.

I want to write a picture book but am no good at illustrating. Do I need to find an artist?

No, but do provide any artwork instructions that are necessary to the story. If a publisher accepts your manuscript they will team you up with an artist from their list. It's highly unlikely that you will ever meet this artist but you will be sent proofs and sample artwork to check.

What length should my children's book be?

It depends on the age group for which you are writing. As a general guide, picture books should be under 1,000 words, preferably around 500. Books for ages five to six are 1,000–1,500 words; six to seven are up to 4,000; seven to nine are up to 10,000; nine to twelve are at 20,000 plus; and teenage books are 40,000–55,000 words.

If an editor likes my idea, will they work with me on my book?

Not unless you have a fantastic idea and your writing shows great skill but needs a bit of polishing. Editors are busy people and receive hundreds of manuscripts every week. They don't have time to rewrite your story for you.

How long will it take me to earn a good living as a writer?

Probably never. There are not that many children's writers out there who earn a lot of money from writing alone. Many supplement their writing by teaching, doing school visits, critiquing manuscripts and other services. Many others have a day job. If you want to write a children's book because you are hoping to get rich, forget it. Write because you have to; because stories are constantly fighting for space inside your head; because writing is what you want to do most.

Should my story always have a moral in it?

Obviously you have to write responsibly when you write for children but you should never preach and any moral in the story should come about as a result of the story, and not be the reason for it. So write a story, not a lecture.

How can I be sure that the publisher to whom I send my book doesn't steal my idea and get another writer to write it up?

New writers often worry about this but no reputable publisher would ever do this. However, it's amazing how often writers come up with similar ideas – I've often seen this with my writing students. So, if a publisher rejects your book about a magic cow that can fly, saying they already have a similar idea in the pipeline, and a few months later they publish a book about a magic pig who can fly – no, they haven't stolen your idea, they really did have another book in the process of publication. It can take two years from signing a contract to a book being published so the publisher will have a lot of books in the pipeline that you don't know about.

My book keeps being rejected; should I send it to a critique agency?

If you really believe in your story, have checked it over and over but still can't understand why it keeps being rejected, then sending it to a critique agency might be worth considering. You will get a professional and objective opinion of your work from an experienced editor/writer, which could help you revise it enough to sell it. On the other hand, you could pay for a critique and your work could still be rejected. If you want to follow this route, an internet search will provide you with a list of agencies. Check out their websites carefully, compare rates and testimonials, and choose the one that appeals to you most.

Is it worth entering writing competitions?

Yes, it's good practice for you and encourages you to write with an aim in mind. Most competitions have some criteria as to word length and genre so will provide good experience at writing for a certain market. If you win, it will be a great boost to your ego and you might even be able to use your story as a basis for a children's novel.

RESOURCES

Useful websites

UK Children's Books (www.ukchildrensbooks.co.uk/pubs.html): A list of the websites of UK children's publishers.

Children's Book Publishers (http://comminfo.rutgers. edu/professional-development/childlit/ChildrenLit/ publish.html): Details of some American publishers and information on writing in general.

Publisher Global (www.publishersglobal.com): Information and websites for publishers globally.

Authors Den (www.authorsden.com): A website for authors and readers.

The Society of Authors (www.societyofauthors.org): A useful society for authors to join as they will vet contracts and give you advice.

The Society of Children's Book Writers and Illustrators (www. scbwi.org): News, competitions and conferences for children's writers and illustrators.

Writing World (www.writing-world.com): Lots of information on writing.

LoveReading4Kids (www.lovereading4kids.co.uk): Reviews and information on current and new children's books.

Red House Book Club (www.redhouse.co.uk): Great for research as it gives details of bestselling, new and popular children's books.

Achuka Children's Books UK (www.achuka.co.uk): Information about children's books, publishing and authors.

Wordpool (www.wordpool.co.uk): An informative and supportive website for teachers, parents and writers.

Scattered Authors Society (www.scatteredauthors.org): A group of children's authors who have all been professionally published. They welcome new members as long as they have a contract in place with a traditional publisher or have been traditionally published in the past.

Writer Beware (www.sfwa.org/for-authors/writer-beware): The well-known website that warns of all kinds of literary scams.

Preditors and Editors (http://pred-ed.com): Another well-known website providing information about literary scams.

Blogs

Here are the names of some blogs you might enjoy reading:

Girls Heart Books (http://girlsheartbooks.com): A daily blog by a team of published UK and Irish authors for girls aged eight to fourteen.

Picture Book Den (http://picturebookden.blogspot.co.uk): A daily blog by published picture-book authors.

Awfully Big Blog Adventure (http://awfullybigblogadventure. blogspot.co.uk): Children's authors from the UK share thoughts on books and writing.

Authors Electric (http://authorselectric.blogspot.co.uk): A blog by a team of fifteen published children's authors, who have chosen to self-publish their ebooks, many of which have been published traditionally and are now out of print.

Stroppy Author's Guide to Publishing (http://stroppyauthor.
blogspot.co.uk): A 'guide to publishing' blog by children's
author Anne Rooney.

Heartsong (www.nicolamorgan.com/category/heartsong-blog):
A blog with lots of useful information by children's author
Nicola Morgan.

Bookwords (www.writingthebookwords.blogspot.co.uk):
Musings by children's author Linda Strachan.

Ann's a Writer (http://annsawriter.blogspot.co.uk): Musings by
children's author Ann Evans.

Children's books mentioned in this text

A Swift Pure Cry, Siobhan Dowd (David Fickling, 2006).

Thirteen Reasons Why, Jay Asher (Razorbill, Penguin USA,
2007).

Junk, Melvin Burgess (Andersen, 1996).

Forbidden, Tabitha Suzuma (Random House, 2010).

Harry Potter and the Philosopher's Stone, J. K. Rowling
(Bloomsbury, 1997).

Can't You Sleep, Little Bear?, Martin Waddell (Walker, 2005).

Where the Wild Things Are, Maurice Sendak (Red Fox, 2002).

I Want My Potty!, Tony Ross (Andersen, 2012).

There's a Pharaoh in Our Bath, Jeremy Strong (Puffin, 2009).

Astrosaurs Academy, Steve Cole (Red Fox, 2008).

Rainbow Magic series, Daisy Meadows (Orchard, 2003).

The Secret Kingdom series, Rosie Banks (Orchard, 2012).

Artemis Fowl, Eoin Colfer (Viking, 2001).

The Snail and the Whale, Julia Donaldson (Macmillan, 2004).

Totally Lucy series, Kelly McCain (Usborne, 2008).

Dead Boy Talking, Linda Strachan (Strident, 2010).

His Dark Materials trilogy, Philip Pullman (Scholastic, from 2007).

My Best Fiend, Sheila Lavelle (Puffin, 1995).

Captain Underpants, Dav Pilkey (Scholastic, 2012).

Just Don't Make a Scene, Mum!, Rosie Rushton (Piccadilly, 2005).

How to Write Really Badly, Anne Fine (Methuen Children's, 1996).

Dolphin Song, Lauren St John (Orion, 2008).

I Was a Rat, Philip Pullman (Yearling, 2004).

Crowboy, David Calcutt (Oxford University Press, 2008).

Fishing for Clues, Ann Evans (Scholastic, 2000).

A Series of Unfortunate Events, Lemony Snicket (Egmont, 2001).

Beast trilogy, Ann Evans (Usborne, 2008).

No-Bot, the Robot with No Bottom, Sue Hendra (Simon and Schuster, 2003).

Ketchup Clouds, Annabel Pitcher (Indigo, 2012).

Maggot Moon, Sally Gardner (Hot Key, 2013).

Darke Academy series, Gabriella Poole (Hodder, 2009).

Dinosaur Cove series, Rex Stone (Oxford University Press, from 2008).

Animal Ark series, Lucy Daniels (Hodder, from 1994).

Horrid Henry series, Francesca Simon (Orion, from 1994).

Mr Gum series, Andy Stanton (Egmont, from 2000).

Skating School series, Linda Chapman (Puffin, from 2010).

Girls FC series, Helen Pielichaty (Walker, 2009).

The Lord of the Rings, J. R. R. Tolkien (George Allen and Unwin, 1954).

Wind on Fire trilogy, William Nicholson (Egmont, from 2008).

Vampire Dawn series, Anne Rooney (Ransom, 2012).

My Secret Unicorn series, Linda Chapman (Puffin, 2004).

The Cat in the Hat, Dr Seuss (Random House, 1957).

The Wind in the Willows, Kenneth Grahame (Methuen, 1908).

Watership Down, Richard Adams (Rex Collings, 1972).

Rotten Rejections, Andrew Bernard (Robson, 2002).

Twilight, Stephenie Meyer (Little, Brown, 2008).

Tweet Right and *Write a Great Synopsis*, Nicola Morgan (Kindle, 2012).

Make an eBook, Michael Boxwell (Greenstream, 2011).

Become a Writer: A Step by Step Guide, Ann Evans (Greenstream, 2011).

My books mentioned in the text:

I Don't Eat Toothpaste Anymore! (Tamarind, Random House, 1993).
And Me! (Tamarind, Random House, 2008).
The Gold Badge (HarperCollins, 1995).
The Amy Carter Mysteries (Top That!, 2008).
Quick and Easy Plays for Primary Schools (Hopscotch, 2007).
Perfect Summer (Astraea, USA, 2013).
Firstborn (Kindle, 2011).
All Aboard! (Parragon, 2008).

Reference books

Personally, I think a writer can never have too many reference books. Here are some titles you might find useful.

365 Ways to Get You Writing, Jane Cooper (How To, 2012).

Brewer's Dictionary of Phrase and Fable (Cassell, 1959).

Creative Writing, Adèle Ramet (How To, 2010).

Eats, Shoots Leaves, Lynne Truss (Profile, 2007).

How to Write a Children's Picture Book, Andrea Shavick (How To, 2011).

How to Write Your First Novel, Sophie King (How To, 2010).

I Before E (Except After C), Judy Parkinson (Michael O'Mara, 2007).

Likely Stories, Hugh Scott (How To, 2012).

Oxford Dictionary of Quotations (Oxford University Press, 1941).

Research for Writers, Ann Hoffman (A & C Black, 1992).

Roget's Thesaurus (Penguin, 2004).

The Children's Writers' and Artists' Yearbook 2012 (A & C Black, 2011).

The Five-Minute Writer, Margret Geraghty (How To, 2009).

The Hero with a Thousand Faces, Joseph Campbell (Fontana, 1993).

The Oxford Dictionary of Classical Myth & Religion, Simon Price and Emily Kearns (eds) (Oxford University Press, 2003).

The Writer's Journey, Christopher Vogler (Pan, 1999).

Write for Children and Get Published, Louise Jordan (Piatkus, 1998).

Writing Children's Fiction: A Writers' and Artists' Companion, Yvonne Coppard and Linda Newsbury (Bloomsbury, 2013).

Writing for Children and Getting Published, Allan Frewin Jones and Lesley Pollinger (Hodder, 1996).

Writing for Children, Linda Strachan (Bloomsbury, 2008).

Writing for Children, Pamela Cleaver (How To, 2010).

Writing magazines

These magazines aren't specifically for children's writers, but you might find them helpful.

Writers Online (www.writers-online.co.uk): Home of both *Writing Magazine*, which is available from WHSmith and other newsagents, and *Writers' News*, which is only available by subscription.

Writers' Forum (www.writers-forum.com): Website of a creative-writing magazine, which is available at WHSmith and other newsagents or by subscription.

The Bookseller (www.thebookseller.com): News of the book industry, with additional children's bookseller supplements twice a year. Available by subscription.

Books for Keeps (http://booksforkeeps.co.uk): A bimonthly, independent UK magazine that reviews children's books and publishes articles on children's writing.

Red House Book Club (www.redhouse.co.uk): Online bookstore with reviews and information on the latest children's books to be published.

Index